I0596799

THE SHREDDED VEIL MYSTERIES

LEAH CUTTER

KNOTTED ROAD PRESS

CONTENTS

The Shredded Veil Mysteries

ISBN: 978-1-64470-025-9

Published 2014 by Knotted Road Press
www.KnottedRoadPress.com

Interior design copyright © 2019 Knotted Road Press
www.KnottedRoadPress.com

Come someplace new...

Are you a traveler? Do you enjoy exploring strange new worlds, new cultures, new people?

Journey into the various lands envisioned by Leah Cutter.

Sign up for my newsletter and I'll start you on your travels with a free copy of my book, *The Island Sampler*.

I will never spam you or use your email for nefarious purposes. You can also unsubscribe at any time.

http://www.LeahCutter.com/newsletter/

INTRODUCTION

The first story in this collection, *Hell By Any Other Name*, was written as the first short story in a challenge: to write, edit, and publish a short story a week, every week for thirteen weeks. (This became the *Baker's Dozen* collection.)

I had known I wanted to write a ghost story. I had gone out with someone the night before, and had ended up talking a lot about ghosts. When I woke up the next morning, most of this world was in my head: Andy, the shredded veils, and Betsy.

I knew what Betsy was from the very first story, though her true nature isn't revealed until the fourth story.

I didn't know what Andy was until the very end of the last story.

I don't know if there are any more stories for Andy, Betsy, and Toni. Never say never, but the arc feels complete to me.

I hope you enjoy their journeys as much as I've enjoyed writing them.

Leah Cutter
October 2012

HELL BY ANY OTHER NAME

I woke up from my nightmare sitting straight up in bed.

If I could sweat, I'd be drenched. If I had a heart, it would have been beating hard in my chest. If I could breathe, I would have been gasping.

I'd been dreaming of Hell, of course.

Most ghosts, if they admit to sleeping, dream of Hell. It was why we were ghosts. That door to the Beyond wasn't full of pearly gates and choirs of angels. No, it was fire, heat, and chaos.

There were a few ghosts who stayed on Earth even though they were promised Heaven. They were all nuts.

I pressed my hands against my eyes, as if I could shut the images out and wipe them away. No luck. I groaned. Quietly. I didn't want any more complaints from Mrs. H— downstairs about unearthly noises.

I was lucky enough to be able to rent a place outside Ghosttown, to live among the living. Even if it was little more than a glorified closet, with only a skinny, single bed and two stacks of crates holding a door across them that served as my desk. Dark water stains marred the formerly white walls, while mysterious lines crossed the ceiling, shadows of discontent.

The only bright spot was Betsy, my camera, sitting in her corner of the desk. Most of what a ghost sees is muted, grayed, behind the veil still. Betsy always appeared red and glowing, as if a warm heart beat behind her dark lens.

That was all my room contained—one of the advantages of being a ghost. No need to cook or use a bathroom. You couldn't really change your appearance, and since you didn't actually have a body, well, nothing in, nothing out. We still needed rest, though. The brain needed time off to process.

I looked at the clock. Two in the afternoon. I caught myself before I groaned again. Flames of Hell still licked behind my eyes if I closed them. There would be no more sleep for me that day, though I didn't usually rise until sunset.

I slid aside the heavy drape covering the window, exposing an inch of daylight. I was in luck. Another rainy Seattle day greeted me. I decided to go to Volunteer Park. Might even go to Lakewood Cemetery. Not because I wanted to greet the newly dead; there was a committee for that. Or even to look at the portals, to see if they'd changed. I didn't believe those myths, that I might somehow do enough good that I'd earn Heaven.

No, it was merely a matter of wanting some company of my own kind. I hated to admit it, but sometimes I got lonely. I rose and walked out into the gray haze of the day, the rain sliding through me as if I wasn't really there.

I tried to think of it as a cleansing, inside and out, but I never really feel *clean*.

DECEMBER 21, 2012 HADN'T BEEN THE END OF THE world, only the Great Unraveling. The veils between the Seen and Unseen worlds shredded.

The living suddenly discovered they weren't alone.

Luckily for our side, we had a lot of lawyers. The Interspecies Act passed relatively quickly for Congress, guaranteeing the rights of the dead and others.

Of course, law and practice were often worlds apart. Seattle had one of the stronger lobbies, though. I praised their work again as I got on the bus, the new card system beeping when I passed my hand over it, automatically deducting my fare. I'd hated walking everywhere before.

The bus was mostly empty. A homeless man slumped on a seat next to the back door, arms wrapped firmly around his pack; two students sat next to each other madly texting, probably to each other; and a professionally dressed man with round glasses and a briefcase on his lap sat stiffly in his seat. He stared straight ahead, his face frozen.

As if he'd seen a ghost.

I almost sat next to him, but I'm not generally that vengeful. It's part of what ghosts do, though: scare the living, whether we mean to or not. The ghosts who get off on it were also the ones who, as kids, pulled the wings off flies, and as adults fired people for a living, know what I mean?

Instead, I swayed as the bus turned another corner, making my way to the very last seats in the back, looking out the window and watching the gray day slide by. I could have gone out in the sunshine. Sometimes I enjoyed seeing the world brightly lit, even though it didn't seem as vivid as when I'd been alive. I missed the feeling of warmth, though. And intense sunlight made ghosts less substantial. People no longer saw me. Instead of trying to avoid me, they stepped *through* me. There was no feeling more wrenching than your former intestines momentarily misplaced.

The man with the briefcase got off at the same stop I did. I didn't think anything of it, since he walked straight ahead when I turned left, into the park. I walked up the winding hill, sticking to the sidewalk, not wanting to take a chance on slipping on the wet grass. Red, orange and yellow leaves lay scattered across the green lawn. I remembered, when I was still alive, how colorful the fall leaves were, how a gray day made them seem more vivid. Dying cast a fog on everything. Nothing was as clear as it used to be. The edges weren't as crisp; the colors, more muted.

I looked through the black donut sculpture at downtown and the Space Needle, and then walked around the reservoir— I'd been alive when it had still been full of water, one of the last open reservoirs in all of Washington. Now it was just a thin pond full of fat koi, algae and bird droppings. Finally, I decided to head north to the cemetery. Walking along the avenue of beechnut trees I saw the man from the bus again. This time he stared straight at me. The hand holding his briefcase was clenched tightly, almost white. With a determined stride, he drew closer. "Andrew Collin?"

"How do you know my name?"

"I need your help."

My mouth must have been gaping because I closed it with a snap. "I only work during business hours," I told him sharply.

"But—"

"If you know my name you already know the address of my office."

I turned on my heel and deliberately walked *through* the nearest tree.

Of course, I appeared on the far side of it. While it was unpleasant for me, I've been told it was distinctly unsettling for the living.

I walked without pause to the cemetery. Only paid professionals among the living ever went there anymore. New memorial parks had sprung up, where the living could go to honor their dead. As a result, cemeteries were one of the safest places on earth. I'd heard stories of more than one attempted robbery or rape ending when the victim fled to a graveyard.

Ghosts could be very vengeful.

Most people avoided graveyards, though, because of the

portals, the doors to Heaven or Hell that surround the places of the dead.

The living saw them differently, as shadows, or else they felt them when they walked too close, a chill that went through bones and into the soul. The doors weren't meant for them. Some got glimpses, though, of their afterlife, whether it was angels or seventy-eight virgins or a blessed nothing. The living couldn't pass through. Whatever they saw was disturbing enough they rarely ventured near.

One of the good things about the portals showing up was that all the mass graves were suddenly findable, even in the middle of the jungle. Murderers now had to be very careful where they stashed a body. Portals stuck around even after a soul went through.

Like all ghosts, I found myself drawn to them frequently. We were *meant* to go through. But some could ignore the siren's call better than others.

Flamed licked out of the nearest portal, drawing my attention. A black, churning cloud boiled beyond the burning edges. The only time I felt heat was near that fire. There wasn't a smell of sulfur, or cries of the damned. Just fire I knew would burn my ectoplasmic flesh, and a chasm that would chew up my soul until there was nothing left.

In an abstract manner I admired the contrast between the comforting trees of the park, the dramatic gray of the clouds, and the shooting flames dancing in the portal. I took another step forward, then another, fascinated against my will.

Maybe if I stared long enough, a pattern would form. Maybe I could find a path through the darkness into the light.

Maybe if I wished hard enough, I, too, could grow wings and fly.

I stopped myself in time, before I stepped through, as I always did.

That Hell was not for me.

I wasn't surprised when the guy with the briefcase sat waiting for me in my tiny office in Ghosttown. The door was unlocked, and the living couldn't or wouldn't touch most of the artifacts in the room.

Still, I looked around carefully to make sure nothing had been disturbed. Papers and notebooks, Fixed so that both the living and the dead could touch them, sat stacked in neat piles on the rickety desk. The beat-up file cabinet in the corner, which I kept not only locked but charmed, stood untouched.

Natural artifacts that I'd found—rocks, keys, broken rings, dried flowers, and other knick-knacks—covered the shelves of the cinder block-and-board bookcase that ran along the one wall, exactly in the same pattern as I'd left them. Each of them held a spark of *something*: life, Heaven, energy, I didn't know. All ghosts collected these things. Some Fixers, those among the living with one foot in the world of the dead, used natural artifacts to create other artifacts, electronics and other useful manufactured items dragged far enough out of the Seen world that ghosts could use them, like Betsy, my camera. Other Fixers said it was a lot of hooey.

Me, I just felt better with the natural artifacts surrounding me.

The guy sat stiffly in the guest chair next to the desk. I had to walk past him to get to my own large captain's chair. I made sure to walk by closely, so he could feel the chill that all ghosts emanate.

"What can I help you with, Mr...."

"Potter," he provided. "Harry Potter."

"You're joking, right?"

"My parents were—whimsical."

Though Mr. Potter wore round glasses similar to his namesake, that was where the likeness ended. He looked more like a Danish architect, with perfect blond hair, starched shirt, classic thin blue tie, and charcoal suit.

"So what can I do for you, Mr. Potter?" I picked up the cracked glass fountain pen I kept on the desk and twirled it in my fingers. I'd been a smoker as a young man, and though the ability had disappeared when I'd died, the cravings hadn't.

"Have you heard of Disruption stones?"

"Of course." Every ghost had. Supposedly, they were strong enough to disrupt your fate: if you threw one into a portal, it would change from an image of Hell to Heaven.

"Mine was stolen. I want you to get it back," Mr. Potter said primly.

I couldn't help it. I had to laugh. "First off, why would I believe you? They're just myths. Next, even if I did believe you, why would you come to a ghost to retrieve it? Why wouldn't I just take it for myself?"

"Most of the myths about them aren't true," Mr. Potter explained. His voice took on a lecturing tone. "They're manufactured, not found or mined. They must be Fixed to an individual, like an artifact. They're horribly expensive, both in time and materials. Like an artifact, only a ghost can touch one. However, only the ghost of the person it's been made for can use it."

"So, someone stole something useless from you," I stated, still not believing him.

For the first time, Mr. Potter showed a streak of anger. "More myths," he said darkly. "Some people erroneously believe they can re-Fix a stone. That a strong enough Fixer can realign it. They're wrong, of course. The thief will destroy it by attempting to change the Fixing."

"Mr. Potter, I investigate missing people, or cheating husbands or wives. I collect evidence for the court. I don't specialize in artifacts. There are others who do. Let me recommend—"

"I don't want *them*. I want you. I investigated you. Thoroughly."

"Really," I said in my driest voice. I had practiced the tone, working to keep out the ghostly overtones.

Mr. Potter paled only slightly, so I thought I'd mostly succeeded.

"You were a cop—"

"Detective," I growled.

Mr. Potter swallowed, then continued. "Detective. With an impressive close rate."

"Not all of those cases were closed cleanly." The Interspecies Act had ensured that the dead weren't necessarily prosecuted for crimes committed while living.

Lots of lawyers on our side.

"You also go that extra mile now," Mr. Potter added. "A very satisfied client list."

"A confidential list of clients," I said, glancing again at my locked file cabinet. Two weeks prior I had noticed something off when I'd come in, as if the locking spell had started to slide. I'd assumed at the time that the spell for shocking anything that physically touched the metal had worn off and I just needed the building Witch to reapply it.

I couldn't be paranoid enough, it seemed.

"People talk," Mr. Potter said with a fake smile. "Particularly with the right monetary incentive."

I bristled. "And you think that will work with me?"

"Triple your normal fee? Yes, I do."

"I won't be bought." Criminals had discovered that early, and I'd carried the habit into the afterlife.

"I'm not asking you to do anything wrong or illegal. Merely to retrieve an artifact that's mine and has been stolen from me."

"Why should I take your word that it's yours?"

"Here's the name of the ghost who stole it," Mr. Potter said. "And the man who paid her." He slid a piece of paper across the desk.

I recognized only the first name. Toni Hermino. Beautiful Italian immigrant. She'd been a thief when she'd been alive, specializing in exotic gems and jewelry. Now that she'd passed over, she focused on artifacts and art.

"Go talk with her. Verify my story. Check me out as well. As an extra incentive, when you return the stone, I'll share the list of ingredients needed to make a Disruption stone for yourself."

I scoffed. "Just the cash is fine."

I didn't believe in this mythical stone. Mr. Potter did. He was seemed to be an intelligent businessman, not given to flights of fancy. Either someone had snowed him good, or there was actually something to this myth.

"I'll pay Toni a visit," I said grudgingly. "But that's all I'm agreeing to do for now."

"Wonderful," Mr. Potter said, his smile full of teeth.

Fortunately for me, he wasn't the only one with a bite.

———

THE HAUNTING HOUR ART GALLERY DIDN'T OPEN UNTIL midnight, of course. I spent the time at one of the Fixed terminals in the library, cruising the electronic highway that ran easily through the Seen and Unseen worlds, investigating Mr. Potter and his nemesis. The three other terminals were empty, their screens glowing with that odd half-light of the almost there. Though the living still manned the desks, mostly ghosts wandered between the stacks, seeking treasures they'd missed in their youth, answers for their unending existence.

Mr. Potter, I learned, worked as a long-term investment banker for the dead. Believe me, there was no one more committed to long term than a ghost with no fear of dying. He'd done well for himself—nice Craftsman on Queen Anne Hill, second cottage out on the San Juan Islands. Divorced, no kids, mother in a very expensive, private nursing home. No charges, no official investigations, not even a letter of complaint.

Squeaky clean.

Something about him still set my ectoplasm crawling.

I arrived at the gallery soon after it opened. The long windows cast brilliant light out onto the dark street. More people than I'd expected clomped across its hardwood floors: some sort of open house. The living walked in groups of two or three, clutching wine glasses and making hushed commentary.

I wouldn't call the images on the walls "art." The drive to create such things, that passion, belonged solely with the living. This was a façade. To me, every piece looked the same, like chalkboards badly cleaned, with squiggling green, glowing lines drifting across them. As a line crossed a boundary of a piece, it turned into smoke and dissipated.

There were very few ghosts who were once artists: no matter their destination, anything was better than a pale existence.

Toni chatted with two guests, accepting their studied praise for the show and the artist. I waited patiently as Toni drew pledges of donations from them for a dubious charity.

I didn't say anything or try to warn them away. I wasn't a detective anymore, and as ghost, it was hard to make a living.

"So, *paisano*, what can I do for you this wicked evening?" Toni smiled like she meant it. She'd probably been stunning when she'd been alive. Now, she was as pale as all of us, her beautiful dress just a shade different than her skin, still clinging to nice curves and shapely calves accentuated with high heels.

"Just checking on a rumor," I told her. "A myth."

"Myth? You? I thought *polizia* were only concerned with facts. "

I didn't bother to correct her assumption. Once a cop, always a cop. "Sometimes disproving something is as important," I said smoothly.

Toni cocked an eyebrow at me.

Maybe not that smooth.

"I've heard...rumors that maybe a precious stone was removed from a magician's house. Care to comment?"

"Ah. If, perhaps, I knew of the possibility of such a thing, how would you show your appreciation?"

I pressed my lips together and rocked back on my heels. I'd expected Toni to deny everything.

It meant she wanted to tell me something.

A too-human laugh interrupted my thoughts. We both looked at the source then looked away.

The dead rarely laughed.

"A favor," I said, rolling the dice. "Big or small. Some future claim."

"Interesting," Toni said, but she was already nodding. "Yes. A future favor it is."

Toni grew pensive and stepped forward, her voice a hitching whisper. I easily caught it, whereas anyone living would draw away from the sibilant, haunting tones.

"A precious stone, such as what you're asking about, if it exists, would be cold, so cold. A little piece, like that," she said, holding up her fingers and indicating a mere inch. "Very heavy." Her eyes took on a distant look. "It was—it would not—be right. Not natural. Not good."

Toni glanced up at me out of the corner of her eye. "Removing such a thing from its owner might not be bad, no?" She ended with a shrug.

I shrugged back. "Depends on who got it next. What they plan to do with it."

At that, Toni smiled. "Such a person might be very arrogant. They might think they can change the nature of the thing. They'll just destroy it. No harm done."

"What if someone was hired to bring the stone back to the magician?"

"I would call him a fool," Toni said coldly.

When I said nothing, Toni nodded her head once, sharply. "I have guests waiting," she told me, looking away.

"Thank you." I turned and headed toward the door, ignoring the whispering humans.

"The magician's castle—" Toni called from behind me.

I paused.

"It's more dangerous than the rest."

When nothing else seemed to be forth-coming, I nodded my thanks and left, walking out of the brightly lit gallery and into the dark of the street. Of course the night didn't hide me— no, here I was more visible. I had my own glow, like all ghosts after midnight.

I wished I could change my clothes, somehow. Pull up my collar. Tug on my sleeves. Something to give myself a sense of protection.

I didn't want to go through with this job. Mr. Potter was a snake. I knew I should walk away before he stuck his fangs in me.

However, I couldn't shake the feeling that something else was going on. A bigger game.

This part of the magician's story had checked out. Now it was time to go see the arrogant man.

MR. A——, SHORT FOR ARROGANT, AS TONI HAD SO APTLY named him, lived only a few blocks away from Mr. Potter, even higher on Queen Anne Hill. A quaint, brick wall separated the yard from the sidewalk, while the yard's sloping incline separated the house from its neighbors, giving it the impression of a feudal castle snubbing those beneath it. It was done in pseudo-Tudor style, with wide, dark planks separating the white stucco. More than one gable peered darkly over the expanse, sticking out from the steeply slanted roof.

The garden was immaculate, of course, the hedges trimmed with tweezers and the grass probably not merely cut, but each blade filed to a precise angle.

Ghosts generally hung out in one or two places in a house

like Mr. A—'s: up in the attic, snuggled into the rafters and listening to the rain, or deep in the cellars.

I'd brought Betsy with me on this trip. Generally, I used her only for photographing cheating husbands or stealthy wives, but Betsy had other talents as well.

The Fixer I'd used for Betsy had been new to the business. She'd had to try more than once to bring Betsy "over" so that I could use the camera. The Fixer had spent a lot of energy, and hadn't charged me much money, because neither of us had realized what she'd done until much later.

She'd made Betsy into a spectralgraph.

As easily as I took pictures of humans, I could also take pictures of things such as houses or cars—anything manufactured—and see any residual spectral effect.

I took pictures of the houses next to Mr. A—'s first. I needed to make sure there wasn't any environmental influence. I seemed to be in luck. This part of the hill hadn't been declared holy, nor did it contain an ancient burial mound. If it had, every house in the vicinity would have a low-level spectral reading.

Then I took a picture of Mr. A—'s place.

It was lit up like the Castro District on Halloween.

Which meant either it was ghost central, or it housed not just a few, but an entire museum's worth of powerful artifacts. As I hadn't seen another ghost anywhere on the street, I had to assume the latter.

Caution told me to wait until broad daylight, when I could approach the house unseen, hidden by the sun.

I told caution where to stick it and climbed the stairs up to the house. That was when I had my first big shock.

The house was *Sealed*.

Not just the doors and windows locked, no. Every bit of folklore, both the things that did and didn't work, were employed around the perimeter. A band of salt, at least half a foot wide, had been drawn in a circle around the property.

Rowan branches rested on every windowsill. Ba Gua mirrors hung over the door. Bottle trees flush with blessings and curses were planted every few feet.

Why the Hell hadn't Toni warned me about *this* place?

I slowly circled the house, counter clockwise, seeking a crack in its protection.

Nada.

In the back, where the neighbors couldn't see, additional protections had been laid: a sticky rope web that had been Fixed. Dancing spectral lights guaranteed to confuse the more weak-willed. Running water from a fountain rolled past half the house like an old fashioned moat.

I had no idea if the house held just as much protection against the living as well. I had to assume it did. I also had to assume that the security cameras mounted every few feet had also been Fixed and were now tracking me.

I had to get out of there before they released their equivalent of Hell hounds.

The moat drew me back. The flowing water had to come from somewhere; a pump, deep inside. It wasn't a naturally flowing spring. Down, underground, it was being recycled. The circle would be broken there.

A light came on, shining out a second story window above me.

Without thinking, I sank *down*, into the ground.

SCIENTISTS WHO HAVE STUDIED THE PHENOMENON HAVE reported that ghosts take on different shapes underground. Some become snakelike; others, more of an amorphous blob.

Me, I've always felt as though I grew round, with a hard skin, like a ping-pong ball. I didn't lose myself or any consciousness, but I know I was very different underground than above it.

Black dirt slid easily around my compact form. Roots parted before me like a tangled curtain. An earthworm blindly kept pace with me as I burrowed through the rich loam.

I couldn't see anything—at least, not in a human sense, with eyes. I was as sightless as the worm. But I sensed that sliver of a crack before me, like a door just barely ajar, its light spilling out into the darkness. It drew me like the sun draws a seedling, that single bright spot in the unending night.

Coldness bracketed me as I eased inside, my natural form tumbling into shape. I stood, stretched, imagining my vertebrae cracking in relief, though I didn't feel anything, actually. I almost groaned, but stopped myself just in time.

The room I'd landed in had piles of boxes against the walls. One of the bottom ones had broken open, crushed by the weight of the boxes on top of it. Its spilled contents had disturbed the delicate chalk lines drawn across the floor, a gypsy sigil to keep out the undead.

I skirted the edges of the drawing, pressed up next to the boxes. Whoever had drawn this had known what they were doing. When I reached the door, I snapped a couple of pictures of it with Betsy. Someone, somewhere, probably knew how to break this one from our side.

The hall I stepped into was as plain as the room I'd just come from. It had been recently painted, with a yellowed linoleum floor and doorways lining the walls. If I'd been thorough, I would have looked in each room, taken pictures of the spells I was sure I'd find there.

But the room at the end hummed with power. I didn't need Betsy's eye to tell me powerful artifacts lay behind it.

Ghosts looked the same, felt the same, every damn day of their existence.

As I drew closer to this room, the hairs on the back of my neck rose up. An actual shiver went down my spine.

It was too seductive for words.

I walked straight through the door into the room without another thought.

Of course, a sigil lay just on the other side. I'd blundered right into it. Caught like an ant in amber, I couldn't move, couldn't sink into the ground or mist away. I was held right there until someone came and freed me.

I tried to compose myself. A security camera had turned deliberately toward me and held me in its sight. Might as well see what was here. Shelves held row after row of artifacts and Fixed items. I didn't recognize any of them, just felt their power. I looked for a stone, anything that might have felt "heavy" or "cold," but nothing struck me that way. Or rather, no stone did. There was a doll's hand that felt "off" to me, and some brown, curled leaves that shifted as if unseen bugs crawled over and under them.

I ignored the first twinge I felt in the center of my back. I was still too busy gawking like some damn tourist.

The second one came with the wonderment of pain.

How was that happening to me? I looked down at the lines drawn in raised chalk. The design appeared to be a standard Chinese holding spell.

Another pain wracked me, this time starting in my gut.

Only then did I really notice the second artifact that had swung in my direction when I'd stumbled in. At first I mistook it for a camera, but no, it was actually some kind of gun.

Like the Disruption stones, rumors of these sorts of things had been around forever, some sort of technology that could be used to banish a ghost.

I struggled wildly then, trying to get free. I'd been banished before. It wasn't fun.

This time it wasn't the abrupt pain of being shoved from the world. No. This was a pulling, like being quartered with Clydesdales, slowly but inevitably tearing each limb off and away.

I bellowed, shrieked, and moaned, causing the very foundation of the house to shake, but to no avail.

I was torn asunder.

I became corporeal—or at least, a ghost again—in the graveyard where my bones lay buried.

Betsy, of course, was gone.

All the portals sprang up, showing images of flame and chaos as I rose. I ignored them and the false comfort of light they provided in the darkness. They looked less out of place than the sign for the cemetery itself. Who puts a flashing neon time-and-date sign at the entrance of a graveyard?

Buses had long stopped running, and no cab would ever pick up a ghost. I started the long walk back downtown. I longed for a cigarette, anything to break the monotony of walking. Though I could move more quickly than the living, it was still going to take a damn long time.

I thought about my options as I trudged back to the city.

Go back to Mr. A—'s and retrieve Betsy. Not practical. Probably not possible. But I'd miss her. She'd been my only touchstone in this existence.

Find Mr. Potter and tell him I'd failed. Then I'd be out my fee as well as my camera.

I couldn't think how Toni might be able to help. She'd already warned me. I didn't have a thing she wanted, I was certain. And I already owed her a debt. I certainly couldn't pay her to go steal Betsy back for me.

With the sun rising, Hell's bells sounding in the blazing light, I was too tired to think anymore. I went back to my room instead, collapsing on my bed and hoping that something besides nightmares would come in my sleep.

This time I dreamed of being banished and never able to

come back, floating amorphous above the graveyard like a lonely cloud.

I can't say it was an improvement over dreaming about Hell.

———

BY MIDAFTERNOON I FINALLY DECIDED I'D HAD ENOUGH OF pretending to sleep. I was still no closer to a plan of action. Mr. A——, of the impenetrable house, still had the Disruption stone, and given the number and strength of the other artifacts he had, I was almost ready to believe that myth.

And now he had Betsy. Her usual seat on my desk looked naked without her. This place was still a dump, barely room to walk, a mere mattress on a rusted iron frame, but it was where I hung my hat, and Betsy made it, if not home, at least mine.

I knew Mr. A—— would have either fixed the crack in his defenses or he would have widened it, placing a trap on the other side.

That didn't stop me from going back there when I realized that the clouds had burned away, leaving miles of blue sky and bright light.

After a bus ride of being trampled on and brushed through, I felt exhausted and out of place. I didn't stop my groan when I looked up that steep hill I was going to have to climb. It wouldn't be physically tiring, not as it might have been when I'd been alive. It took will, though, and I'd been pushing myself for a while.

The Puget Sound shone blue beneath the hill, boats and ships, large and small, skimming across it. Wind I couldn't feel swirled the dried leaves on the sidewalk. I couldn't smell the air, but I knew it would be crisp and clean.

The fake Tudor house looked the same as the night before: dark windows, perfect lawn, graceful walk—

—that led to a gaping-open front door.

I told myself it was my former detective instincts kicking in.

Mr. A— was far too paranoid to leave his front door open. Something had to be wrong.

Honestly, though, I just wanted a way into that house.

I raced up the path, flowing as fast as the wind, when Mr. Potter stepped across the threshold. He shook hands with Mr. A —, the pair of them laughing.

I couldn't help my low growl. They appeared to be on very cordial terms.

I pushed myself into bush next to the walk. Twigs rammed through my gut and lungs, branches pinned my arms. Though I didn't need to breath, my lungs felt constricted, as if there weren't enough air. If I could sweat, despite the cool day I would have felt it trickling down my forehead and back. I made myself stand very still, blending into the bush, fading with the light.

Though Mr. Potter wore different glasses that day—white rimmed, very European—they didn't help him see me.

Or he never would have brought Betsy out of his bag.

I WAITED UNTIL FULL NIGHT BEFORE I WENT TO BEARD THE magician in his own den. I wanted him to see me this time. I'd wasted away the rest of the afternoon in a park, sitting on an isolated bench facing the trees. No other ghost came by, just a wind that made the living shiver and the trees dance. I had no arguments planned. I just wanted to finish this. Get Betsy and run.

Of course, it wasn't going to be that easy.

The windows of Mr. Potter's house that looked out over the street were leaded in the upper part: old glass that ran with time, looking heavier than it ought to. When I drew near, I figured out why. Mr. Potter's house had protections similar to Mr. A—'s. Someone had drawn lines of protection around every gray shingle on the walls as well as on the lead of the windows. Knotted rope lay against the foundation, salt infused to its core.

I walked around the house, keeping to the stone walkway, not daring to step off it in case there were other traps I didn't see.

The crack in the house's protection was deliberate. The door to the root cellar had been left bare.

No choice but to go in that way. I flowed through the door but didn't step onto the floor. Who knew what kind of sigils had been engraved there?

However, I was overly cautious. The neat tile floor of the laundry room held no chalk, paint, or dried chicken blood. A navy blue washer and dryer sat in one corner and Mr. Potter sat in a chair next to them, reading something on a tablet. "I've been expecting you," he said, putting his reading material down and standing. "I need to pay you the rest of your fee."

"You lied to me," I told Mr. Potter's retreating back.

"Not a big lie. Not really. Toni did steal the stone from me, to help me shore up my defenses. Mr. A— had bet me that no one could beat his, which more than made up the fee I'm paying you."

Only then did Mr. Potter realize I hadn't followed him. I'd seen too many sigils and curses in his buddy's house. I wasn't going to be caught again.

"Don't you trust me?" Mr. Potter said, seemingly aggrieved.

"No, I don't. Now give me Bet—my camera. And never contact me again."

A loud, human groan came from behind the door Mr. Potter had opened. He gave me an odd half-smile. "That might be someone hurt. You should go see."

I stayed where I was. If there was a person in there, I couldn't do anything for them. I couldn't touch them. Chances were the presence of a ghost wouldn't comfort them, either.

Another groan slithered through the air.

"Damn it. Potter, what are you playing at?"

"Come see," he said, beckoning.

I should have left. Hell, I should have *run* as quickly and as far away as I could.

The third groan ended with a pained whimper.

Obviously, I had more humanity left in me than Mr. Potter because I flowed into the room.

A skinny, bearded man lay on a long table pushed against the far wall. His clothes were mismatched and filthy; he was probably homeless. He'd been stabbed in the gut. Blood pooled over the hands he had clenched to his abdomen. From my years on the force I knew it was already too late. He was bleeding out.

The door behind me slammed shut. Of course, the room was *Sealed*. Not a single crack that I could escape through.

"Hey, buddy," I said to the homeless man. His eyes were glazed over and he couldn't see me. Couldn't hear me. I reached out my hand, but I knew if I tried to touch him with it, it would just sink through him.

"What now, Potter?" I asked, looking around. A single window sat high above me, with an ancient shoot underneath it. This used to be the coal room, I realized. More recently, it had held the firewood for the house. Split logs lay in neat piles across the other wall. A handy ax leaned against them.

I couldn't touch or manipulate anything in the room.

"Now, you leave." Mr. Potter's voice came in clear over hidden speakers.

"Afraid you're going to have to open the door," I told him. The floor was cement, but had been reinforced with lead and was impossible to sink into.

"I don't have to. He will."

The homeless man coughed once, a death rattle. Hollywood has tried to emulate that sound for decades, but they'd never come close to the real thing. It was enough to give a ghost chills.

"Your kind is wrong," Mr. Potter continued. "You should all be forced to go Beyond, where you belong."

I hadn't taken Potter for a bigot. He worked for the dead.

No—he worked for their *money*.

"You don't really care about us, ghosts or the dead," I told him. "You just want to keep everything you've stolen from them. That's why your house is so protected, as well as Mr. A—'s. Your pious act is justification for your petty crimes."

Mr. Potter chuckled. "Very astute. However, my crimes are far from petty. You've seen my accounts?"

I had, as well as the contracts that signed everything over to his firm once the dead did pass Beyond. Shaking my head, I replied, "Petty." Ghosts never trusted the living completely. "None of them have given you full access to their resources."

"But the promise of a Disruption stone makes them much more amenable," Mr. Potter said smugly.

I scoffed. "Still a myth."

"No, I have—ah."

The homeless guy on the table had finally died.

I'd never seen a spirit rise before. This, I learned, Hollywood had gotten right. A younger, better-dressed version of the man sat up, pale and, well, ghostly, while his body stayed on the table.

A portal to Heaven sprang up instantly. All bright blue sky and endless green fields—some kind of pastoral afterlife.

Would have bored me to tears. Still. Lucky bastard.

Without even a glance in my direction, he swung his legs down and walked straight through.

As soon as he'd passed, the portal turned black. Flames lined the arch and clouds gathered.

I finally realized I was doomed.

Mr. Potter had laid a clever trap. My only way out of this room was through that. Eventually I'd crack. Potter knew it. I couldn't resist forever, not in a locked room, not with that constant siren's call.

"Let me out, Potter," I told him one last time, unable to tear my eyes from the flames now licking outside the doorway.

"Go back where you belong," Potter hissed.

"See you in Hell," I said.

Then I moaned.

I closed my eyes and put everything into it, giving voice to my unearthly displeasure.

"What are you doing?" Mr. Potter said.

He didn't sound panicked. Not yet.

I moaned, repeatedly, louder and louder, sending waves of sound through the foundation of the house, through the walls, shaking the core of all who heard.

"Stop!" Potter screamed.

I didn't.

Mr. Potter had forgotten that ghosts are creatures of the dead.

Though we prided ourselves on adjusting to modern life, at our core, we still did one thing best: haunting the living— terrifying them.

Sometimes to death.

A RINGING KNOCK ON THE DOOR FINALLY MADE ME SCALE back my yowling. I didn't know how long I'd been there, singing the songs of the dead. The flames of the portal danced in time with me, cackling hellfire, pleased, I think, with the terror I'd rained down.

An officer whom I'd met when I'd been alive stuck his head in the door. "Hey, Andy."

"Ed."

He took out his earplugs, then led the way out of the room and upstairs. He spoke as he walked. "Potter ran into the street and directly into an oncoming car. He's at the hospital now. Unconscious. They don't know if he'll regain consciousness." Ed didn't look at me.

I hoped the bastard died while dreaming of my haunting.

"The whole thing is taped here," Ed told me, leading me

into Mr. Potter's study and showing me the four large plasma screens on the desk. "We know it was self-defense. You'll still have to come down to the station and give a statement."

"Fine by me." Potter's study didn't hold as many artifacts as I thought it might. The only one I wanted to see was Betsy, and there she was, waiting for me.

Ed didn't say anything as I scooped her up.

He couldn't see the small, heavy rock sitting next to her, or how I picked it up as well.

BY THE TIME I FINISHED AT THE STATION, LATE AFTERNOON had come again with familiar clouds and rain. I had the officer drop me off at Volunteer Park and made my way directly back to Lakewood Cemetery. I walked through the wet grass, remembering its former brilliant green. More trees stood bare now—must have been a storm the previous night. I nodded to a few of my fellow ghosts, whispering to each other near a grave, then made my way alone to a bench where I could watch the flickering portals.

The stone weighed heavily in my pocket. Cold, too, like a frozen piece of night.

Or maybe not night, but nightmare.

Pious didn't buy you Heaven. Being a bastard didn't necessarily mean Hell, either. You had to believe in good, as well as do it, was the theory of the day.

Me, I'd been a pessimistic bastard all my life, as well as far into my death.

I don't know why I tried to change my luck. When I walked to the nearest portal it flickered, growing dark. I watched the unending flames, the hungry clouds, then finally tossed the stone inside.

Unlike a real stone, it didn't land on the other side, but stayed somewhere Beyond.

Nothing changed until I turned to go.

Suddenly, sunlight shone through the gateway. My beloved city of Seattle lay stretched out on the other side. My heart ached to be there, to go *home*. Even without stepping through, I knew it would be perfect. I would know everyone I met, and if I didn't, they'd still be friends. There would be good food and wine, endless talk and laughter interspersed with quiet time in the hills and on the water. There would be books and time to read them, music and dance whenever I wanted.

I still walked away.

It wasn't mine. I hadn't earned it. I couldn't be bought. Not then, not now.

I turned back to the gray Seattle day, knowing I'd never win that clean, beautiful city...but that I still had to try.

TO HELL AND BACK

I HATED WORKING IN THE DAYLIGHT. NOT BECAUSE THE sunlight burned ghosts. Quite the opposite, in fact: I couldn't feel the heat, and the bright light washed me out, leaving me invisible.

Do you know how annoying it is when the living stopped stepping around you, and instead, stepped *through* you? I swore my intestines had started dancing on their own, a sloshing, gurgling feeling that left me seasick.

However, I had a job to do and a wealthy client to please. I was following her canny bastard of a husband. He had just enough knack or luck to keep losing me.

First, I waited for him downtown, outside of his office building. The day would have been beautiful, if I'd been alive and able to enjoy it. Fall tinted the air cool and crisp, and the trees still held onto their burning colors. I could see ghosts better than the living, but I only saw two others the entire time I waited. They were all sensibly sleeping through the day, waiting until evening to rise.

The bastard showed up at noon, when the living filled the streets as if a bell had sounded, releasing them all from their pens. I struggled against the tide to chase him, the number of arms, legs and shoulders passing through me disorienting. I overshot where he'd turned off and raced back, only to find him stepping onto the only light rail car that wasn't Fixed, that is, dragged somewhere between the Seen and Unseen worlds, so that I and my fellow ghosts could interact with it, not pass directly through it. Luckily, I got on the next one, close to the door, so I could watch and make sure he didn't slip by me again.

He got off at the University, and I was able to follow him directly for at least a street. Students walked in gaggles, not droves, so I was able to step around them, and only got a backpack swung through my shoulder for my effort.

Of course, my own luck didn't last.

He met his lover at a seedy motel, just off 45th. It had classic architecture, with two levels of rooms and a walkway facing the parking lot. The building itself was stained amber, and neon palm trees surrounded the welcome sign, as if they were following a southwestern theme. She was already waiting for him, and hid behind the door as she opened it, not that I was in place or ready with Betsy, my camera.

The habits of the living died hard. You didn't start acting like a ghost immediately after you died. It took time. For me, it took at least twenty minutes before I remembered that I didn't need for them to open a door for me to enter a room.

I could go through the wall.

Since I wasn't collecting evidence for a court case, but just for my client, the bastard's poor wife, it didn't matter how I got it, illegally or not.

The bastard's luck proved stronger than mine, though. The motel had been built in the '50's, when lead paint was still *de rigueur*. The room was effectively *Sealed* against my kind.

I walked back out to the parking lot. At least it was quiet, no one passing through me. But I was bored. I'd always been bored on stakeouts when I'd been alive, and working as a detective. But at least then I had convenience store coffee and stale donuts to distract me.

Finally it occurred to me that I might be able to catch them in the act if I could just get them to open the door.

I weighed the two artifacts in my pocket—a sliver of clear, green glass, as well as a small stone. They were found artifacts, each with a spark of energy or Heaven or *something* that carried them out of the Seen and into the Unseen world, tiny pieces that ghosts as well as the living could touch. I didn't want to lose them.

I also didn't want to lose my client.

With a practiced throw I hurled them against the hotel door, one after another. Each gave a satisfying *thud*, sounding as if someone had just knocked twice.

The bastard opened the door sooner than I'd expected. Fortunately, I was ready and got the perfect long shot, him with his tie still undone, her, still rumpled and naked in bed.

"What do you want?" he demanded.

I quickly looked around. He couldn't have been addressing me. I stood in full sunlight. None of the living should have been able to see me.

He turned his head, following another being. I snapped as many shots as I could as the thing ambled off. It looked something like a ghost, but faded, as if not even here in this world. Even I had problems seeing it.

I took a few more long shots of the guy and his squeeze before he shut the door on their love nest.

I printed the entire series, both with the ghost as well as the happy couple, paying extra to have sigils drawn on the back of each, so I could touch them. I'd never seen anything like the faded being. He, I think it was a guy, had wisps trailing from him, like he was unraveling or dissolving. I had no idea what had happened to him.

Of course, when I showed the other pictures to my client, she turned on me, as it were my fault her husband was a cheating bastard. Seemed I was supposed to have come up empty handed, not prove his deviltry.

Not for the first time I was glad I was a ghost and had left such passions behind.

I AVOIDED MY OFFICE FOR THREE DAYS AFTER THAT. I SETUP blocks on my email after my client flooded my inbox. I would have stayed away longer, but there's only so much graveyard haunting a ghost can do.

When I walked in, I nearly walked out again.

Beautiful Antonia Hermano sat waiting in my guest chair. Since becoming a ghost I didn't have blood that could heat, a heart that could beat faster, or other parts that would appreciate such a beautiful woman.

Still, the habits of the living died hard.

"Andrew, *paisano*, so nice to see you again," she said, standing so her chest rose first. Her hand twitched, almost coming up to shake mine before falling gracefully to her side. Ghosts couldn't touch each other, any more than they could interact with most of the Seen world.

"I was thinking this office was a scam and you never come in," she scolded as she sat back down, crossing her long legs demurely. Her dress didn't ride up, one of the advantages of being dead, though she could never change it or adjust it either.

"I was busy," I told her, still standing by the door. I glanced to the side, but I couldn't really think of a good enough excuse that would allow me to escape. Nothing in the office had been disturbed either. The file cabinet in the corner was still locked and charmed, and the rows of artifacts on the bookshelves sat in the same careful arrangement I'd put them in.

"The living can be so trying, no?" she asked, giving me a coy smile.

I pressed my lips together and nodded, my defeat clear. She

knew I was no longer actively working on a case. I walked further into my office, resting on the large captain's chair behind my desk. "What can I do for you Ms. Hermano?"

"Toni, please," she said with what probably had been a killer smile when she'd been alive.

"All right, Toni, how can I help you?" I asked, keeping the sigh out of my voice. If she was bringing out the smile so early, it was going to be bad.

"You remember the magician? And his stone?"

Grimly I nodded. Toni had been paid to steal a precious artifact from a banker named Harry Potter. The theft had been a ruse. The stone hadn't been. I squashed any regrets I might have felt about not taking my one chance to step into Heaven.

"You promised me a favor in return for my help."

"I remember," I said, bracing my self.

"I need you to go find my brother, Beppe, Giuseppe. He's stopped emailing, I can't get in touch with him."

"Living or dead?"

Toni gave the closest thing a ghost could to a laugh. "You flatter me, thinking I'm young enough to have a living sibling. He's dead, of course."

"And he hasn't just moved Beyond?" I asked, skeptical. Some ghosts got tired of resisting the siren's call of the portals. Even though all they showed you was Hell, sometimes it was damned hard to go on existing.

"No, no, he's still in Yakima."

"Yakima? You want me to go to Yakima? That's—"

"What a good friend would do if they were owing a favor," Toni told me archly.

"But it's days away!" I complained.

"Only hours by car."

"Which I can't afford."

"Of course, if you don't help me, I will just have to explain it to all the other ghosts in my neighborhood why I'm so depressed."

I nodded, knowing when I'd been beat. "No reason for you to be despondent. I'll take care of it." The ghost community was small, and I needed them more than I needed my dignity. "So he's just gone missing?"

"No, not according to his old boss, also dead. He claimed he'd seen Beppe yesterday. He was worried, so worried he emailed me. Beppe seemed—faded, like a ghost who was only half there. Have you ever heard of such a thing?"

"No," I said, instantly lying. "I haven't." I thought back to the ghost I'd photographed, how unhealthy he'd seemed.

"Maybe it's a kind of exotic spell or something," Toni mused. "What do you think?"

I shrugged. "I don't know."

I was afraid, though, that I was going to have to find out.

As a ghost, I had two options for getting from Seattle to Yakima. Hire a private car and driver, which I would have insisted on if this were for a regular client, with regular expenses.

Since this was on my dime, that meant public transportation.

It wasn't that I didn't know how to drive—I'd had a car when I'd been alive and it wasn't a skill you suddenly forgot once you'd died.

The problem was that it was illegal for ghosts to drive. Though our side had plenty of lawyers, we'd lost this one.

Bridges over running water were the primary problem. Each end of the bridge needed to be Fixed. The cheapest way was to attach an artifact or two to each end. They couldn't be imbedded in the concrete, just glued on.

Imagine some bored teenager, who ignored all the hexes and warning signs around the artifact, and merely pried it loose. Or maybe the original Fixer was in an accident and died, which automatically lessened all of his or her spells, possibly even negating them.

Now imagine that along came a ghost, driving. As soon as they hit either end of the bridge, they'd be stopped. They wouldn't be able to go any further.

The car, however, would have no such difficulty, and would continue driverless until it crashed.

I took the light rail out to the airport. I remembered when the cars were new. I couldn't smell the musty seats but I could see the decay, the glass etched with tags, a layer of grime covering the seat backs, all the poles aged with ten thousand hands, grabbing at them.

At the airport I waited alone. I didn't even see another ghost in the terminal. Ghosts rarely traveled. It was uncomfortable for us to be too far away from our bones. All the bright advertisements surrounding the ticket counter were for the living.

When I approached the bus, the driver waved me off. "Whoa, there. Where do you think you're going?" He looked down the length of his reddened nose at me, his eye as watery and gray as the skies.

"Yakima," I told him, showing him my ticket.

"I can't take you! My bus isn't set up for your kind."

"According to the Interspecies Act, all public transportation must be made readily available for those who require it," I intoned at my driest.

The guy rubbed the back of his neck. "Look, I don't want any trouble. But I can't take you."

"Go check your office," I told him. "Maybe you have an artifact there that you can use." I may have growled a little. His eyes shot up to mine and though he'd grown a little pale, he straightened up to his full height, so he could look down on me. "There's no need for that."

"Then Fix your bus."

The guy walked away shaking his head. I started wondering

how long it would take for me to get to a public phone, if Dean would be around and if he'd be interested in this kind of case. The Defender's office had a lot on its plate right now. I doubted they'd hear my case for months.

Finally the driver came back a bright star in his hand. "You were right," he said. He looked over his shoulder. A woman in the company's uniform stood there, her arms crossed over her chest. She gave me a nod. "We don't want no trouble," he added. "I just have to stick this in the storage compartment, under there," he said waving.

"Put in on the ceiling in there," I told him. "I'll sit on the seat directly over it."

He nodded then went to the very back of the bus and stuck it there.

Rosa Parks wasn't one of us, unfortunately. I sat in the back, separated from all the other passengers. Fortunately, ghosts don't have a great sense of smell, so being that close to the toilet didn't bother me.

The sound of the engine did, though. As a ghost I didn't have a body, so I didn't get headaches. The noise still grated on my nerves, making me grumpy and tense before we'd even left the city.

It got worse.

I'd forgotten how each mile between me and my bones dragged on my soul. I could hear the women a few seats ahead of me exclaiming how beautiful the mountains were, how brilliant the orange trees stood out in the forests of conifers.

I couldn't see it. The colors registered, but not their vivid nature.

My soul grew heavier as we moved further into the pass, the mountain and all that rock weighing it down. I struggled to stay quiet. It would be too easy for the driver to "lose" the artifact fixing the bus if the other passengers started complaining about unearthly noises.

The air dried out on the other side of the pass. Though I

didn't need to breathe I still felt my chest tighten. We moved further away from the rain that cleansed me, inside and out. The hills looked naked, bleached gray with dust and age, covered in barren rock.

Two military helicopters kept pace with us as we went through the final set of hills, from Ellensburg to Yakima. I'd forgotten there was a military base out here. Ghosts, even former commanders, couldn't be counted on rejoining. Patriotism didn't stir a dead heart: not much did. Plus, troops wouldn't fight beside them. No matter how conditioned a soldier was they couldn't operate efficiently beside the dead. We made the living either too cautious or too foolhardy.

So ghosts and the military didn't mix, despite all the rumors of secret weapons, drugs and super spies. I wondered again what exactly I'd gotten myself in to.

TONI'S VERY NEAT INSTRUCTIONS INCLUDED STREET NAMES and turns. She hadn't bothered to mention that the vineyard sat at the top of a hill, steeper than Queen Anne.

I didn't bother keeping my groan to myself. There wasn't anyone I could disturb out here in the middle of nowhere. I'd been damned lucky the bridge leading to this road had been Fixed.

I thought about flowing up the hill, cutting across the brambles and dried thorns, taking my chances on the loose rocks and dirt. Decided to take the road and its switchbacks instead—both were going to take effort and I already felt drained. It was late afternoon, and I'd only slept a little on the bus ride out: too distracted by each mile between me and my bones.

Crucified sapling—apple trees with their branches splayed open—lined the dirt road to the vineyard. Wooden crates sat piled in front of them, full of blood-red fruit. At least a dozen workers rapidly picked apples out of the mature trees, filling their overly large aprons. I saw a few ghosts there, wandering lost between the trees. But Toni had specifically said the vineyard, so I moved on.

The wine tasting room sat on top of yet another hill. I paused, gathering my will to go on. I suppose the valley was pretty, with the trees still decked in their autumn colors, the fingers of pink clouds reaching out from the sunset, and the vine stakes arranged like grave markers across the valley.

More ghosts flitted around the edges of the vineyard. When I looked carefully, I saw three half-ghosts, the ones who seemed even more out of phase with the world. They were easier to see in the dimmer light of the evening, though they didn't glow like a normal ghost should.

As I was about to enter the vineyard one of the almost ghosts stepped out. "Hey," I called to him.

He didn't seem to hear me, kept shambling away.

I followed him. "Hey," I said again, getting in front of him so he stopped.

Dead eyes raised to meet mine. A distinct thrill of fear went through me. "What—what happened to you?"

The ghost smiled at me, turning that delicious, momentary feeling into revulsion. He was guileless, thoughtless. Whatever personality gave him cohesion was *gone*. For me, all I saw was a living Hell.

"Not just happening," he insisted. "Is happening."

"What?"

"The Slide. Away and away and away."

As if he'd forgotten I stood there, the guy ambled off.

Ancient ghosts—and there are a few, millennia old—had held onto their wits better than this guy. It wasn't age that had done this, but something else.

I rapidly walked along the edge of the vines, looking down each row for more ghosts. Though the vines didn't grow that high, something about how they were placed made it difficult to see the ghosts. Finally I saw a group standing at the far end. I plunged into the row, the dead leaves of the vines crackling as wind I didn't feel picked up.

When I drew closer I saw that two of the ghosts in the group were normal ghosts, and one was faded. The two argued with him. I couldn't hear what they said but I recognized the antagonistic tones.

I also recognized the third ghost. Toni had been right to be worried. "Beppe," I called, striding up.

His two companions took one look at me and walked away.

Beppe stood alone, forlorn, with the same idiot smile as that other first ghost. Like Toni, he'd been genetically blessed with good looks: broad shoulders, a strong jawbone and a royal nose. Most ghosts come to Earth clean: no matter what condition they'd been killed or buried in, ghosts tended to wear their Sunday best and looked like they'd had their Saturday night bath.

However, Beppe had grape stains on his fingers. He'd really loved his life.

"Hey, *paisano*," Beppe called, his words slurred. If I didn't know his body couldn't process alcohol, I would have said he was drunk. He swayed, listing to one side. Then he looked up again. "Wait. Do I know you?"

"Antonia sent me," I told him, watching as he swayed to the other side. "Beppe, let's sit, okay?"

Without bothering to look for a bench, Beppe collapsed to the ground as if his strings had been cut. "Antonia?" he asked, his head in his hands. "Where is she? Is she here?" He looked up, then around, barely staying upright even though he was seated.

"No, no, she's still in Seattle."

"Ah. Seattle. With her art and her life."

I didn't bother to correct the last part of that.

"She's good, no? A good sister. Whereas me—" Beppe

heaved an impressive sigh for a being who didn't actually breathe.

"What happened to you?" I asked as gently as I could.

"If I told you, I'd have to share," Beppe said slyly.

"Share what? Not that I want any," I hastened to assure him. I didn't have to fake my shudder. I wasn't interested in trying whatever it was that had done this to him.

"Not gonna slide any to you," he said, cracking up.

Ghosts never laughed.

"Get it?" Beppe said. "Slide?"

That was the second time I'd heard that word. I took a guess. "Where are you getting the Slide?"

"Shh," Beppe said, the sloppy shushing of all drunk men. "It's a secret." He purposefully looked up at the sky. "Can't say. They'll know."

Either he was being overly paranoid about the military presence in the area, or not paranoid enough. Only time would tell. "Come on, let's get going," I told him, standing.

"Where to?" he asked, stumbling to his feet.

"Where ever it is you sleep," I told him. I figured if I could get him home, maybe I could get him sobered up.

"No, no, I sleep here, my friend," Beppe said, awkwardly lowering himself back to the ground. "Between the vines. So I can see the stars."

I looked up and shuddered. Too much sky for my taste. Give me a city and light pollution any day. "What about those other two ghosts I saw you with? Will they leave you alone if you sleep here?"

"No." Beppe affected another sigh. "They say I'm a disgrace. That I should step Beyond. They are not understanding like you, my friend."

I actually agreed with them, but I wasn't about to tell Beppe that. We each chose our own Hells. "So they don't Slide? They don't like Slide?" I wasn't sure how to use the slang.

Beppe cracked up again.

Ghosts laughing. It was just wrong.

"Naw, they don't Slide. But you will, my friend, next time?"

"Next time when?" I asked Beppe, watching as his eyes closed.

"Tomorrow," Beppe said, nodding. "Tomorrow and tomorrow and tomorrow." He giggled. It sent shivers up my spine.

I turned to go, leaving Beppe to what were probably better dreams than mine ever were. The good news was that he was already dead: I didn't have to wait with him and turn him over, in case he threw up.

"Wait, where you going?" Beppe asked. He pushed himself halfway up then flopped back down, giving a proper ghostly groan.

"I've got to go see a guy. I'll be right back."

Beppe nodded. "Okay. I just—don't want to lose you. So many don't come back up. Slide right through the gates." He gave another moan, sad and low, the voice of mourning. "Slide just helps 'em—slide away. You know?"

I didn't know. But I was going to see if I could find out.

"Tomorrow, Beppe," I told him.

"Tomorrow and tomorrow and tomorrow," he said.

Normally, in full night, you could see a ghost. We had our own glow. Beppe barely registered against the dark ground. He looked more like a translucent shell than a full ghost. Still, there wasn't anything more I could do for him here.

I needed to get to the library, to do some research. However, instead of aiming toward the main road going back into town, my body turned unerringly toward Seattle, as if I was a bird aligned with the magnetic poles. I knew exactly where my bones lay. I ached, deep in my soul, in a manner I'd never imagined possible.

I made myself walk back toward Yakima instead.

I could have gone home. I'd fulfilled my promise to Toni: I'd found her brother, and seen the trouble he was in. I'd never promised to fix it. Yet, here I was. I blamed my human existence and my cop instincts.

A worm grew in the heart of this lush valley, and I meant to find it.

I DIDN'T WANT TO BE RIGHT. THE NUMBERS ON THE screen flickered in the half light, as if ashamed of themselves. I pushed back from the library desk, wishing I could at least fake one of Beppe's huge sighs.

The ghost population was decreasing rapidly. Normally it stayed at an even percentage, a golden curve. In the last six months, though people still died and the usual numbers became ghosts, they weren't hanging around.

I doubted they were all suddenly finding Heaven.

"You done?" asked the greasy-haired teenaged ghost waiting for my terminal. He bobbed his head to his eternal music.

Me—I'd manifested wearing my good cufflinks. They'd been my grandfather's. I'd always wondered which of my ex-wives had insisted I be buried in them.

This kid, well, I could see the faint cord of his i-whatever snake up from the neck of his hoodie and into his ears. I wondered what he listened to. He appeared to at least still like it. I also wondered how long that would last. As I can't change my cufflinks, he'd never be able to change his music.

"Yeah," I said, clearing the page and logging out of my accounts.

I decided to go the traditional route first and walked to the precinct downtown. All the historic buildings surprised me—I hadn't realized Yakima was that old. Very few ghosts hung around those, of course. They stayed near the newer buildings, the graves of their old haunts.

The front desk of the precinct was busy, much busier than I

expected, until I realized they were in the middle of processing a whole gang of drunken men.

I hesitated by the open door. The harried sergeant at the desk still caught my eye. "Can I help you?" she asked. Murphy said the name on the counter.

Two of the drunks started shouting at each other, each accusing the other of stealing the last bottle of beer.

She rolled her eyes then looked back at me. "Can I help you?"

"Former detective Andrew Cullen," I said, introducing myself. "Is Detective Lewis around?" I didn't know the man, I'd just looked him up in the police records.

"Robbie? Yeah. You know his wife?" she asked, suddenly curious.

Maybe I should have learned more than his name and that he worked narcotics. Too late now. "Afraid not, no ma'am." Given my luck, I couldn't afford to lie. I was sure to get caught in any I gave.

"Nice lady," Sergeant Murphy said. "Still a bit sensitive," she warned as she reached for the phone.

I nearly groaned. Of course he was.

Before I could stop the sergeant she told me, "He'll be down in a minute."

I stepped back toward the door, wondering if I could make a quick escape.

It was easy to recognize Detective Lewis. He was the only one who walked in, then did a double take.

As if he'd just seen a ghost.

Then he straightened up, squared his shoulders and marched right over to me, his faded brown eyes determined, his mouth set firmly in a neutral line. "Detective Lewis," he said. He made an aborted gesture with his hand, as if to shake mine.

Old habits.

I introduced myself then asked for a moment of his time.

"Of course." One of the drunks suddenly woke up and

started shouting again. "Let's step outside. At least we'll be able to hear ourselves think, eh?" He swung the door open and left.

I could only follow him. I couldn't remind him that it wouldn't be a great idea to chat, outside, at night, with a ghost.

"Do you mind?" he asked, not looking at me as he shook a cigarette out of his pack and started walking up the street.

"No," I told him, keeping my hands firmly by my sides. I hoped that when he died that he'd step through straight to Heaven, because nicotine was an addition that followed you into death.

"So, Detective Cullen—" he said, taking that first sweet drag. I watched enviously.

"Just Andy," I insisted. "Have you heard about a new street drug called Slide?"

For the first time since we'd stepped outside Detective Lewis looked me full on. He blanched slightly. The night here was darker than I was used to, in Seattle. Ghosts have their own glow, particularly after midnight.

Though others, mainly the living, have described it as more of a deathly pallor.

Still, the detective shouldered on. "No. Should I have?"

"I don't know. I don't know if it has any effect on the living."

He paused then kept walking. "Didn't think there were drugs that affected you lot."

I shrugged. "Might be new."

"So it's not illegal—"

"But it should be. It's killing your ghosts."

Detective Lewis came to a full stop at that, his lips pressed tightly together, his jaw stone hard. "You're already dead," he said in clipped tones. "Wouldn't it be better if you went Beyond anyway? You're not really the same, after, when you become a ghost." He stared me straight in the eye, as if daring me to contradict his statement.

I wondered if he was referring to his wife. I had no real

experience. Everyone who'd known me well when I'd been alive was long dead. No one could tell me if I'd changed once I'd passed over.

"Passing Beyond is a choice. It should be a clear one," I told him. We stared at each other, living and dead across an untouchable barrier. Finally he lowered his eyes and started walking again.

"That's what Bea said. Why I had to leave," Detective Lewis admitted quietly. "So she could make her choice in peace."

"I'm sorry for your loss," I told him, the words automatic and comfortless.

"Your loss too," Detective Lewis said with a sudden smile. "Bea was a spitfire. Great lawyer, too. I just wish—" He sighed.

"It was her choice," I told him.

Detective Lewis nodded.

"With this new drug, Slide, ghosts can't make the choice. It's getting made for them." I didn't know that for a fact. I just had two pieces of evidence and I was pressing them together, hoping they'd fit, like a two-year-old with his first puzzle.

"I'll do some digging," Detective Lewis promised, taking one last long drag on his cigarette.

I raised my nose slightly, like a dog seeking a scent. Nothing but the usual, too cool air, pressed against me.

"Come by tomorrow night, I'll let you know if I've found anything."

"Thank you." I paused, adding again, "I am sorry for your loss."

Detective Lewis jammed his hands into his jacket pockets. "I know, really, I do. It would have been just as great a loss if she'd stayed." Then he turned and hurried back to the artificial daylight of the precinct.

While I stayed outside in the dark, cold night.

MY NEXT STOP WAS THE LOCAL DEFENDER'S OFFICE. EVERY city and most towns had one.

I did mention that we had a lot of lawyers on our side, right?

They worked for ghosts' rights, with a passion that few ghosts had. I don't know if they thought they could earn their way into Heaven by working for their fellow beings after death, or if it was simply self-interest, but they'd ensured that the undead had equal rights to the living, whenever possible.

The Defender's office was in old town, farther away from the center and bright lights. It really felt as if the sidewalks had rolled up after 8 P.M. All the offices, boutique wine shops, and artsy craft galleries were long closed.

I expected the Defender's office to be open. It was staffed by ghosts, who were nocturnal by nature.

However, because I have the luck I do, it was closed.

I turned to go—someplace. I wasn't certain. I wasn't looking forward to sleeping outside, either in a park or back up in the vineyard, but I didn't seem to have much choice.

There was another ghost on the sidewalk behind me. He bobbed his head as he walked. It took me a moment to remember the teenaged ghost I'd seen in the library.

I forced down my paranoia. It was a small town. The ghost population was shrinking. I was in front of the Defender's office, a legitimate destination for all ghosts.

Despite that, I still felt my virtual hackles rise.

"It's closed," I told him as he came up.

"Yeah, I know," he said, still moving his head in time with that beat only he could hear.

"You know?"

He nodded. "I also told them you wouldn't."

Rustling behind me made me stand up straighter. I refused to turn around.

A blond man in fatigues stepped out of the bushes next to the sidewalk. He looked like the perfect poster boy for the army, clean and pressed, standing as stiffly as if a plank was tied to his back. He gave a brief nod to the boy, who ambled away, before turning to me. "You've been sticking your nose where it doesn't belong," he told me.

I looked at his insignia as well as his name patch. Either he was wearing someone else's clothes, or he didn't care who knew him. "Private Standish, what are you going to do about it?" He couldn't stop me, couldn't touch me, and I wasn't in some sort of *Sealed* room. His smirk of confidence irritated me.

"You have a choice," Standish told me. "You can come with us, or—" He beckoned one of his cohorts forward.

Another army type, though not as put together as Private Standish. He wore his cap backwards and his jacket open. He also had a gun trained on me.

I nearly laughed. A bullet would go straight through me. Standish's men were more likely to hurt one than me.

Then I looked again.

It was a banishment gun. I'd encountered one of these before. It was a slow, torturous way of dis-embodying a ghost. "Oh," was all I said before looking back at Standish.

"You know what this is," he said, surprised. "Not many do. So?"

I have to say I honestly considered it. The experience was far from pleasant. Imagine your limbs being torn from your body, slowly, painfully, without serration of the agony.

However, I would have reincorporated, or become a ghost again, in Seattle. I could tell Toni I'd found her brother and let her deal with it. I wouldn't have to endure more time with all that bare rock between me and my bones.

At the end, I had to go with them.

There was still too much of the living in me, too much sympathy for the dead.

I FELT RELIEVED WHEN THEY DIDN'T TAKE ME TO THE military base. I didn't want to believe that it was all some government plot. Still, I didn't know for certain until we stopped at a trailer park. It wasn't the fancy one I'd seen coming into town. This one was abandoned. Even had its own Portal to the Beyond flickering next to a bombed out doublewide. It flared to life when I walked by, with chaotic clouds and leaping flames.

The living didn't see them, not really. The Portals weren't meant for them. They were there for us. We're supposed to step through them, into the Beyond.

I just wasn't ready for that Hell yet.

The trailer they took me to was *Sealed* of course. The only opening was a deliberate crack in the center of the floor, carefully marked with a lurid purple sharpie. All the furniture and fixtures had been removed. The six-man crew crowded into the space. I finally got a good look at all but the one still holding the banishment gun on me. They were a mixture of townie and military. Hernandez seemed to be second in command, talking quietly with Standish for a moment before heading further into the trailer.

Hernandez returned with a wide-brimmed bowl, as broad as a sunbonnet. It was made of blue porcelain and filled with a deep, burgundy red liquid that glowed slightly, like merlot that had been Fixed.

The bowl was special. It had been Fixed perfectly. Both the living and the dead could interact with it equally, as opposed to one side or the other having more control. It took a lot of energy for that level of balance. It had also been spelled: my nose twitched from the magic, though from this distance I didn't see any runes or sigils.

Hernandez carefully placed it on the floor, over the crack.

"So the only way for me to get out of here is through that," I said, gesturing.

"No, we'd be happy to banish you," Private Standish said.

A lick of pain kicked in along my spine. It was a unique enough experience that I admit I just stood there for a moment.

"So this is how you get ghosts to do drugs," I said. I wondered how they'd figured it out. All I could think of was that something must happen when a ghost changed form to go underground and that opened us up to more influence, here.

Private Standish laughed. "Oh, no. Ghosts pay for this shit. And pay well. It helps them *feel*."

I shuddered. I understood too well.

A ghost's existence was really never here, on Earth. Every color was diffuse, every emotion, flattened. With this drug, maybe there was that passion again, a simulacrum of heated blood.

I couldn't let myself try it, even once. I'd be hooked.

I walked closer to the bowl. Hernandez hadn't set it down precisely. On the far side, barely a quarter inch of the liquid rested above the crack.

Maybe I could go through that way, without touching the center. How much of the drug did I have to pass through to effect me?

"This came from the army, didn't it?" I asked, stepping right next to the bowl.

"Do you know how hard they tried to get you fuckers to fight? First you wouldn't leave your bones, then you just didn't care."

"I'd always thought you didn't want to fight beside us," I said. "Fighting with ghosts diminishes your moral."

He snorted. "Yeah, that too. But at least the living do as they're told."

"You know, most ghosts kill themselves after trying your drug."

Private Standish shrugged. "So?"

"Seems a bad business plan, hooking your clients on something that decreases your customer base."

"People die all the time. Now come on. Dip your toe in the water." When I paused again, he added, "First one is free."

With that ringing endorsement I focused my intent like never before and went *down*.

NORMALLY WHEN I TRAVELED UNDERGROUND, I FELT AS though I changed into a small sphere with a hard shell, like a Ping-Pong ball. I didn't know for certain. Scientists who had studied the phenomenon reported ghosts took on many different shapes, some long and snakelike, others like amorphous blobs, or even spiraling tops.

As I dipped into the earth I felt my shape encircle me and I pushed myself, getting as far away as fast as I could. However, when the drug hit my system, I started to unravel. Instead of a compact form I trailed sluglike streamers behind me. I had to slow down: I feared leaving part of myself behind and not even realizing it.

The army boys could be following me, but they probably wouldn't bother. They seemed supremely confident that either I'd become an addict, or I'd step Beyond.

Cool soil curled around me. I could almost feel its rich grittiness. I found it distracting, all these sensations, the weight of the ground above me, the silk slide of the dirt I passed through.

I made myself focus. All I had to do was allow myself a single thought of home. Instantly, I could orient myself. I plotted my course by that steady beacon of Seattle, sailing blindly through the ground.

When I felt the space before me thinning, I finally rose. I found myself standing on the far side of the bridge that led to the vineyard.

Dawn was coming soon. The light made my skin prickle. I looked at my hands and cursed.

I'd faded.

I tried to take a breath, emulating Beppe. Couldn't do it. I took careful stock. Everything felt the same, flat and ordinary, mundane. I didn't feel drunk or high or likely to fall over.

Maybe I'd escaped most of the effects of the drugs.

Then the sun rose.

Vivid color sprang back into the world. I had to shield my eyes. The hillside was a multitude of browns, tans, blacks, grays, yellows, reds—every color I could name, and more.

I groaned, heartbroken.

All this beauty that I could never touch.

I trudged up the hill to find Beppe. He talked with some of the workers on the edge of the orchard, giving them directions. He seemed more solid this morning than last night. Maybe the drug was wearing off. Or maybe I'd just been brought to his level.

Beppe's smile quickly turned to a frown when he saw me. "No, no, no, no," he muttered, grabbing at my arm—

—and nearly succeeding.

We stopped and stared. Ghosts couldn't touch anything. Maybe as half ghosts, though, we could touch each other. Or come closer to it, at any rate.

"Tomorrow," Beppe finally said, arms akimbo.

"Isn't tomorrow today?"

"Not without me," Beppe said stubbornly.

"Sorry, wasn't really my choice." I closed my eyes to all the variations of green in the orchard, the soft light shade of the newer leaves, the thick darkness of the mature ones, the spread of green to yellow and red in the leaves that had started to change.

"Army men?"

"Yes. You know them?" I asked sharply, opening my eyes to stare at Beppe.

"No, not the big bosses. Just the little ones."

I had to see if I could get through to Beppe at all. "The drug, you know. Sliding. It isn't right."

Beppe shrugged. "It's Yakima. And the army. There have always been drugs here, carried by them. Always."

I nodded. Even when I'd been alive the city had had its problems. I couldn't think of a way to stop them, not with that kind of backing. I needed to get to the Defender's office. They could take it from here.

"We should go now," Beppe said, smiling slyly at me. "It's tomorrow, you know," he admitted.

How many more times would Beppe be able to take Slide before he slid away? I didn't owe Toni anything more. I still felt responsible.

I knew I'd never be able to talk Beppe out of going back. I fell into step beside him. "Part of the drug comes from the army," I told him, guessing. "But part of it must be made here."

Beppe nodded. "I don't know the full mixture. But I think, I think they use our grapes as well."

"That might explain the color," I said. "What about the bowl?"

"Oh, the bowl," Beppe said. He looked around, as if checking to make certain we were alone on the empty dirt road. "Jorge, he bragged once, he stole some of the Slide. But it didn't work. Not without the bowl."

So I could cut off a head of this dragon, prevent them from plying their trade for a short while, until they got another container. That might give the Defender's office enough time to put pressure on the military.

"I'm glad you're coming with," Beppe said. "To come and Slide again."

I stilled for a moment before I made myself continue forward. "Of course."

I told myself I meant that, of course, I would never touch that stuff again. The colors hurt my eyes, the brightness of the day cut into my soul.

I was afraid that I meant exactly what I'd said—of course I'll take more.

***

IN THE MURDEROUS AFTERNOON LIGHT ALL THE COLORS on the abandoned mobile homes grew lurid. I knew the drug hadn't worn off and was affecting my senses, or at least I hoped that was the case because no creature, living or dead, should have to exist in a home that was that particular shade of puke green. Red, tinged with cotton-candy pink covered the neighboring roof—maybe they'd painted it that color in retaliation. Screaming yellow made up the trim of what could have been a perfectly nice white trailer.

The only normal color was the black of the Portal that sprang to life as we passed. I stopped and stared for a moment, willing to see a change. Nothing. The turbulent clouds belched nothingness, while the flames cackled, hungry for my soul.

My Hell remained.

Beppe came back for me. "Don't look," he whispered. "It's not true."

I took two steps away so Beppe now stood closer to the Portal. The clouds immediately cleared away and an achingly blue summer sky appeared over lush green fields. I could tell the vines were heavy with grapes.

"That is true, you idiot," I hissed at Beppe. "Look at that."

"No, no," Beppe said, stepping away resolutely, looking at the ground. "It can't be."

There had always been rumors of ghosts who had changed their fate. I'd never believed it was possible.

Beppe stepped behind me, so the glorious was replaced with ignominy. "It will be lonely there," he told me stubbornly.

"Only if you want it to be."

"It's not, mature, ripe enough," Beppe said. He looked at

me. The naked *want* on his face sent a shiver through me. "Soon," he promised.

As we walked toward the final doublewide, Beppe added, "The Slide. That's real. That?" He waved behind us. "That fate? A dream. Can turn in a flash." He sounded so earnest.

I knew he was dead wrong. He had to be.

"Beppe, let me go first," I told him as we drew close to the stairs.

"I understand," he said with a grin. "You're eager. That's good."

Eager wasn't quite the right term, but I didn't bother to correct him.

The door to the doublewide stood open. Private Standish wasn't there, but Hernandez was. He looked just as disheveled as he had the night before, his military jacket open, showing sweat stains around the collar, under the arms. His boots were worn, and he hadn't shaved. The other men still treated him like the big boss, though.

"Back already?" he asked with a smirk.

"Well, I really, I really only got a taste," I said, nodding my head, trying to look as nervous as I felt going back into the lion's den.

The bowl already stood out in the open. I just had to get a little closer.

"So whatcha bring us?" Hernandez asked.

"Bring? I, ah, didn't bring anything. Standish had said the first one was free!"

"You already had a first one."

"Not much of one!" I complained, adding a ghostly whine to my voice.

"You are a little bit more here than the others," Hernandez

conceded, rubbing his ear. "Come on. Quick dip then. But next time, a great big fat tip for me, right?"

"Yes sir," I said. I walked closer and moaned again. Some of the sadness and regret I felt was real. I already craved this stuff more than cigarettes. And I was never going to take another hit of it.

The bowl shimmied at the overtones in my voice.

I moaned again.

"Hey, what are you doing?"

Only soldiers had been trained to advance on a moaning ghost. The civilians left. Quickly.

Pain raced down my left side. Someone had focused a banishment gun on me. Wonderful.

I pressed the tips of my fingers against the lip of the bowl, careful not to touch the liquid, and moaned into it. As the pain from the banishment gun grew, I moaned louder, feeding my anguish into my voice. The pain wrenched my soul, tearing my body away.

All the windows shattered. The men cursed and I sang on. Pain no longer filled my vision, but I didn't care.

Finally the bowl crumbled, dropping onto the floor as if all of its fragment could no longer stay together.

Surprisingly, the Fixing didn't immediately fade. I was able to hold onto a piece of the bowl.

"What did you do?" Hernandez asked, advancing.

"Put you out of business," I told him straight.

"For a while."

"Only for a while," I admitted. Before they could hit me with the banishment gun again I streaked away, out the front door.

"Quick!" I shouted to Beppe as I raced by. "I stole some of it for us! And part of the bowl!"

Beppe followed close on my tail. "But we can't go back!" he whined.

"You won't have to," I promised. I flowed to the Portal and threw the sliver of bowl I was holding through it.

I expected it to merely land on the other side, like a normal stone or piece of glass would.

It didn't. It slid, somehow, between the realities. I could see it in both places, in my Hell and this Hell on Earth.

Beppe slammed into me, pushing me forward. I was so surprised I stumbled, barely catching myself on the edges of the Portal.

Hellfire burned my face and a tremendous longing to end it all, to quit, to just go away, overcame me. I couldn't, though. I pushed back and swung Beppe in front of me. "See, not so empty," I told him. "You can slide right through there."

Maybe Beppe would have gone on his own once he saw that, indeed, his precious drug lay on the other side. Maybe I could have talked enough sense into him that he'd see the Heaven in front of him.

Or maybe the only way Beppe would go through is how he did, with my boot against his back.

THE DEFENDER'S OFFICE WAS OPEN THIS TIME. THEY seemed very interested in my case. Detective Lewis was as well. I stuck to heavily populated areas, with lots of ghosts, for the extra day I stayed in Yakima. Didn't want to take a chance that Private Standish might try to find me.

Though if he did, and he used the banishment gun on me, at least it would have saved me the price of the bus ticket.

I found out later that the army, once presented with the evidence, used the men as scapegoats and hung them out to dry. Of course, they disavowed any knowledge of the base components of the drug, claiming that it was all the men's fault, that they'd invented everything.

Rumors of drugs continued popping up in. They were

squashed quickly, and another head was cut off the hydra, nothing more.

I took my weary soul back to the bus station. This time the driver quickly affixed the artifact behind his own seat. He made a joke about how the cold of the grave would make him drive extra carefully.

I couldn't have cared. The Slide was leaving my system and I was crashing hard.

When we reached the pass, after Ellensberg, the rain finally came. I wished I could open the window and stick my head out like a dog, letting the rain clean away the last of the orchard dust and slick drugs.

I slept after that, lulled to sleep by the constant spattering water. However, even asleep I knew when we turned that final curve, when the weight of the mountain lifted off my soul, when it was a clear and easy shot back to my bones.

"I saw him go, Toni," I assured her. We sat in my office, well after the witching hour. Though I'd explained it all in an email to Antonia, she'd still wanted to hear the story directly from me.

The glare she fixed me with could chill even the dead. "You swear it was Heaven."

"It looked like Heaven to me. Blue skies, orchards and vineyards full of fruit." I didn't mention the Slide. Or that Beppe may not have gone willingly. That I'd touched another ghost had been strange enough. I'd given Toni my theory that Beppe had started fading when the Portal had changed to Heaven.

It could have been true.

"Thank you, *paisano*," Toni finally said. "I'm glad someone was there for him." She stood slowly. "You should get some rest. You look pale." She gave me a ghost of a smile.

"I will," I told her, also standing. "I may go home now." There was no real reason for me to spend more time in the office that night. The Slide was wearing off slowly, colors fading back to a normal gray tinge.

Antonia and I stared at each other.

If I'd been alive, I would have asked her out for a drink, or maybe a late night dinner.

As a ghost, I had nothing to offer. Maybe my company, but that didn't feel like enough.

"Good night," Toni said, nodding once before she left.

I stood in the center of my office, alone as always.

The habits of the living died hard.

HELL FOR THE HOLIDAYS

A BLACK CLOUD FOLLOWED ME OUT OF MY ROOM AND INTO the bright Seattle sunshine. It had started small enough, the size of a darkened fist too ready to strike. As I walked down the street, washed out by the light, it grew larger, as big as a baby's head, misshapen and black. Then it grew bigger than a nasty dog, pestering me as I hurried along past deserted houses and dried out gardens.

I couldn't shake the cloud no matter how many empty buses I boarded. When I walked into the cemetery it grew larger as well as more bold. Instead of merely trailing me now it began to actively pursue me, drawing nearer. The cloud started to churn and boil, like the clouds of Hell and suddenly I knew that if I let it touch me, I would get sucked straight to there. There was no way for me to destroy it: fire would bounce off it and burn my ectoplasmic flesh.

Since I was still a ghost, I could streak across the earth, much faster than a human. Or I could go underground, travel through the roots and loam. The damned thing followed me regardless, drawing closer all the time.

I found myself next to the water, hoping that maybe it couldn't follow me there. I sprang onto a Fixed ferry, one with shining artifacts lining the bow so that both the living and the dead could interact with it.

For a while I seemed to have lost it. I tried to enjoy the ride. If I could have breathed I would have filled my lungs with the fresh sea air. I remembered how cool the wind felt on the water from when I'd been alive, despite the bright sunlight.

A sudden bang behind me made me whirl around. The cloud was almost upon me. I could see the Hell it promised me, a bleak nothingness for my soul, where there was no order or understanding, merely chaos and fear.

I backed up, hitting the rail. I couldn't run and I couldn't swim.

The banging came again. The cloud thinned as it spread, big as a blanket, ready to engulf me.

As it swooped toward me the banging noise sounded all around me, and I finally opened my eyes. I was safe, in my room, with only my thoughts to consume me. "Come in!" I called as the banging continued. May as well see whoever had just saved me from my latest nightmare. I glanced at the clock: only 1 P.M. Far too early for a ghost to be rising.

I lay flat on my back staring up at the formerly white ceiling, tracing the spider webs of decay and disuse. Almost every day I woke up and thought I should hire someone to clean it.

Almost every day I told myself not to bother.

The knocking came again. "It's open." As a ghost I had very little that anyone would want, outside of my camera, Betsy. She sat on my desk, the only warm spot in the whole room. When I left her behind, I locked and charmed the door to make sure she was safe.

While I was there, well, only a fool would bother a ghost in his lair.

A youngish woman poked her head into the room. She had dark curls that had been popular in the '50s and were again now. Her clear gray eyes shone with a knifelike intelligence, sweeping the room and doing ten thousand little deductions about my life that were all probably accurate. She had the healthy pink skin of the living, though it held the pallor of an office worker. If I'd been alive I might have called the pea coat she wore Kelly green, but the haze cast over all colors muted it to a mere pastel, with dark pants and leather boots.

"Andrew Cullen?" she asked, looking straight at me as I sat up, leaning against the hard iron frame of my bed.

I nodded.

"Uncle Andy? I'm Susan." At my blank look she continued. "My dad, Billy, was your nephew."

"Grandnephew," I corrected. "Or is it great-nephew? I forget." I pulled out the desk chair—the only other place to sit other than the bed—and pushed it toward her. She stayed standing.

Billy had been one of my brother's second wives' kids. I hadn't seen him, or any of the family, since I'd died.

Susan seemed content to just study me, not saying anything more. "What do you want?" I asked, keeping my voice gentle and all unearthly tones out of it.

"Sorry!" Susan said. Her fair skin colored easily. I wondered what shade of pink I would have called it if I'd been alive. "You look a lot like your photos, of when you were younger. With G2."

"G2?" I vaguely remembered that name but it had been a while.

"Great-grandpa. Your brother. The pair of you dancing at Tom's—my brother's—wedding."

I remembered the wedding, the muggy Minnesota day, how we all sweat like pigs standing for hours in the ancient church that smelled of incense and moldy books, the frigid reception hall at a generic country club afterward, how green the grass of the course had looked, how awful the food had been. I'd danced with Tom, with Billy, with a cute young thing whose name I now couldn't recall but who may have led to my second divorce. She'd been worth it.

"What do you want?" I asked again, adding a bit of a ghostly growl, enough to unsettle the living.

Interestingly enough, that didn't cause Susan to pale.

"I want to help you."

"What makes you think I need any help?"

Susan let her eyes take a slow tour of my room, pausing at the desk that was merely a door on top of cinder blocks, the threadbare bed resting on a rusting iron bedframe, the walls stained with mildew and dirt. Then she returned her gaze to me, a single eyebrow raised.

I shrugged. It wasn't much, but it was home, and better than the crypts in Ghosttown. Why anyone except some Goth-vampire wannabe would sleep in a coffin was beyond me. "You haven't answered my question."

"I want to help you because you were kind to me as a child. Plus, you're family, and it's almost Christmas."

I blinked and counted the days. Christmas was only four days away. It wasn't as if I'd forgotten it was coming—who could with the frenetic ads and aggressive good cheer of the living? But Christmas was just another day for the dead. "Really?" I asked, skeptical.

"You're right. It isn't just you I want to help. Tell me, why are you a ghost? Why haven't you passed Beyond?"

"The usual," I told her cautiously. Almost all ghosts stayed on Earth for the same reason: the portal to the Beyond showed them Hell. Every ghost had their own individual version of Hell, but it was still Hell to them.

"Your Hell, then. What's it like?"

"Why are you here?" I wasn't about to share that vision with such a tenuous relation, let alone anyone else.

"You show me yours and I'll show you mine," Susan said smugly.

"What? The living can't see Hell."

"Not through the portals, no. Do you remember what I do for a living?"

I shook my head. I vaguely remembered some kind of doctorial celebration, but that was it.

"I'm an atomic physicist. Back in 2011 there were some discoveries about how atoms communicated on a subatomic level, which was the start of my line of research. Chicks in the same batch would hatch at the same rate despite one group of eggs being kept colder than the other for a while." She looked expectantly at me, as if I'd recall having read the same physics journal.

"I don't understand," I told her honestly.

"See, if chicks can communicate, why not ghosts? Across the Beyond?"

"Not possible." I'd heard about ghosts who'd set themselves up as psychics, claiming they could talk with other beings through the portals. Charlatans, all of them, but the living wanted to believe.

"Let me show you what I've built. Bring your camera to photograph it. It's an electronic portal to the Beyond. And it's *programmable.*"

"So?" A trickle of disquiet went down my spine.

"I can easily enough show you Heaven as well as Hell."

"Wait, you can generate a portal to the Beyond?"

"Yes. But not just any place, to a random Heaven or Hell. I can show you your own Heaven. Or if you have a friend you want to see again, you merely have to call them and I can show you their place as well."

"So it isn't a portal. I can merely see through it," I said, disappointed despite not believing her.

"No, you can go through," Susan assured me. "I've sent artifacts through, seen them land and stay there, never appearing back here on Earth. Anything living I've put through has died."

I didn't want to believe her. I knew I wouldn't have the

strength to turn away from my Heaven a second time. If it turned out not to be real, if I let my hopes get up only to be disappointed again, I might end up going through a portal anyway, Hell or not.

"Please, you have to come," Susan said. "I want to help you. All of you." Her clear gray eyes shone.

Susan wasn't a snake oil salesman. No, she was something much worse: a true believer.

AT SUSAN'S INSISTENCE I BROUGHT MY CAMERA BETSY, though in the same breath Susan told me I couldn't tell anyone else, emphasizing the confidential nature of her work. She still wanted me to take pictures, though. I wasn't sure why.

Susan's laboratory turned out to be in the basement of her house. From the size and age of it, plus the location in Redmond, I guessed it had probably been built by a Microsoft millionaire back in the 90s, when they'd been young and cashed in their stock options.

The house was more tasteful than some of the mansions I'd seen. It was a fake Tudor style ranch done in taupe and brown. Topiary carefully contained in the shapes of two unicorns, rampart, guarded the door. Porcelain figurines peeked out from the hedge: zombie garden gnomes, hobbits and fairies.

"I didn't know atomic physicists got paid so well," I told Susan as I snapped a photo of the terra cotta fountain splashing in the center of the circular driveway, checking the resulting picture to make sure that only the normal level of spectral residue was hanging about.

"It doesn't," Susan assured me. "I have some generous backers. Plus, this place was in foreclosure. It wasn't that expensive."

"Ghosts," I guessed. Long-term savings as well as compound

interest took on a whole new meaning when you were already dead and not going anywhere for a long, long time.

"And others," Susan assured me. She gestured at the white rock wedge with layers of figures and a castle at the top next to the house. "I haven't done anything to the place—it's pretty much how the former owners decorated it."

That explained the creepy bug-eyed thing who peeked over the unicorn's shoulder, as well as the stained glass window that made up the door: a light, airy castle with a river of blood broiling beneath it.

"Why aren't you showing your investors your portal?" I asked Susan as she cleared away the rowan branches she'd laid across the threshold. I didn't bother to point out that while that myth might be true—the wood would stop the undead from crossing—only sealing a door didn't stop a ghost from coming through the walls or window.

"I have," Susan said with a grin. "Well, a prototype," she admitted.

I could barely pay attention to her explanation of delayed trials and needing more volunteers. A *hum* ran from the fake marble floors through the soles of my shoes and up my legs, a slight vibration that was subsonic and went bone deep.

Only as a ghost I no longer had any bones. I'd never experienced anything like this. Ghosts felt very little physically. I wanted to lay down and spread my arms out, embrace the rare sensation.

Susan didn't seem to notice. She led me through the sunlit but empty living room, past a working medieval fireplace, skirting a grand staircase and down an empty hallway where the hooks for many pictures still littered the walls, to a set of double doors that led downstairs.

Opening the doors increased the vibration. I could now feel it in my chest. If I'd had a heart it would have been beating hard and fast.

"Welcome to the new world," Susan said with a grin as she descended.

I clutched Betsy as I followed, wondering if Susan was Beatrice or Virgil, if she was my tour guide of Heaven or Hell.

THE BEAST DOMINATED WHAT HAD ONCE BEEN THE MEDIA room. The sunken circular row of seats had been pulled out, or eaten by it. Cables and vents growing out of its spine like spikes kept it tethered to the wall. To the other side, where there should have been a gigantic maw, stood an empty doorframe. It looked like the old metal detectors, the security gates you used to have to pass through at the airport, before the imaging technology.

Didn't make me feel any safer.

Susan walked past the beast to a console I hadn't seen. She had both a gesture pad and a keyboard. "I just have to start PETER up."

"Peter?"

" Portal Enhancement Technology and Electronic Replicator. Peter is also the patron saint of bridge builders. Plus the guardian of the pearly gates."

"Really?" I looked at the hulking machine and knew I would never call it something as friendly as "Peter." It was the beast, and would remain so.

"Never bring an atomic physicist to a party. They'll ask questions like, does a radioactive cat have eighteen half-lives?"

I shook my head and snapped a few pictures. As I'd suspected the beast appeared all black on the physical plane, but it had a weird, blue aura that I'd never seen before, lit up like the tree at Rockefeller square.

The vibration under my feet changed pitch, then fell, almost disappearing. A new sensation replaced it—a beam of something, energy, life force, wind from Beyond—started pouring through the empty metal doorframe.

I walked toward it slowly, fascinated despite the literal chills rolling down my spine. White mist sprang up across the threshold, rising to the top of the frame, contained by the arch.

"It's ready," Susan said quietly.

I still saw nothing, not Heaven or Hell, just a cloud filled gate.

"Take a picture of it," Susan suggested.

I couldn't hold back my gasp at the result. Normally, Betsy couldn't capture anything in a portal. I'd tried a few times when I'd first gotten her back from the Fixer who'd made her, after I'd realized that in addition to photos she also could be used to measure the spectral residue left behind by ghosts or powerful artifacts. She never showed even a hint of a portal, all I had from that afternoon were a few nice pictures of trees beyond the graveyard.

This time, Betsy had taken a picture of something else completely: my personal Hell. My stomach turned with the constantly rolling clouds, the raging flames.

"I don't—I can't—" I stepped back from the portal, though I didn't feel the compulsion to approach it like I did with a real portal. When I'd been closer to it, I didn't feel the heat of the flames, or even the cool of her mist. Only Betsy showed the truth of what lay there.

"May I see?"

Numbly I showed her the picture.

Susan's breath caught, but she merely nodded. "Thank you," she said quietly.

I debated erasing the photo. It was irrational, but I hated for Betsy to be carrying around such a sight. Logically I knew it wouldn't corrupt her. I still didn't want it near her. I couldn't email to myself: my encryption was good, but nothing was perfect. I ended up keeping it, planning to download it to a drive and lock it away until I decided to pass Beyond.

"So, now that we have that calibration, let's try something else."

I heard the pride in Susan's voice. I could indulge her eagerness to show off her beast.

"Do you know of a ghost who passed Beyond recently? Someone you felt close to?"

Ghosts didn't feel close to anyone or anything, but I didn't point that out to her. I had known someone, though. "Beppe," I told her. Giuseppe Hermano. I'd helped him pass Beyond, if by help you meant a kick in the pants when he didn't want to go to his Heaven.

"Think about Beppe," Susan instructed as she returned to her console. "I know, I know, it sounds so unscientific and touchy-feely. But at a sub-atomic level you'll be able to reach through the portal to wherever he is. I'll track your call and amplify it. Think of Beppe's Heaven."

I looked sharply at her. "How did you know he'd gone to Heaven?"

"You wouldn't want to look up somebody in Hell."

I nodded. She was right. I thought of the blue skies of Yakima, splayed apple trees bursting with fruit, vines heavy with grapes. I remembered Beppe, who'd loved his life so much he'd become a ghost with wine-stained fingers. I thought of him whole and not faded with the deadly drug he'd been taking.

"Get ready to take a picture. . .now," Susan instructed.

I hesitated, not wanting to contaminate Betsy with more of my Hell. But if it really was Beppe's Heaven, his sister Toni would want to see. So I snapped two, three pictures before I dared to look.

There were the rich fields I'd remembered. The view was from high on a hill, looking down on the valley. I saw more than one person picking grapes: zooming in it was easy to find Beppe, smiling and whole.

"Thank you," I told Susan as I showed her the picture. I'd

wanted to believe Beppe had found his Heaven and left behind the drugs—seeing it made it more real.

"Here," Susan said, sliding a half-screen across the beast's portal doorway. A mesh hung loosely between its uprights. The setting had already reverted back to plain mist, nothing hidden behind it.

"What's that?"

"A spectralgraph, like your camera," Susan said. "I wanted you to see the portal on your own device first so you'd know there wasn't a trick." She paused, then asked quietly, "Want to try to find your Heaven?"

"Yes," I said immediately. "Please." I couldn't remember the last time I'd felt like begging. Probably with my third wife. I hadn't begged for my life. The doped out kid who'd shot me hadn't given me a chance. He'd just gunned me down and run away, my life bleeding out into the alley, no second chance.

"Think of what it might be like," Susan told me. "It might be different than you image, though," she warned.

I didn't need to imagine, I *knew*. With trepidation I watched the rolling mist change into its terrifying form, my Hell springing across the screen, before it drained away like fog, and then it was there.

The view was still odd, high on a hill, but I could see everything: the city, the sound, the libraries and the quiet adventures that awaited me. I could easily imagine all the friends and friends-to-be walking the streets, having coffee or maybe sneaking to an early happy hour. If I could have cried I would have. My soul ached to be there, where I belonged, where I'd always belonged.

I snapped at least half a dozen pictures with Betsy before the vision dissolved. It went through the same sequence in reverse, clouds covering the city like morning fog, changing into black hellfire then cooling into mist again.

"I can't hold the portal open for very long," Susan

apologized. "It's unstable on a quantum level. Or below. I'm still running tests."

"Don't apologize," I told her sternly. "It's—what you've shown me—it's a wonder."

"Then you'll go through?" Susan asked, excited.

"You need a volunteer," I said slowly.

"Yes. To show my sponsors my progress. And my success."

"You know pretty much any ghost would agree after a demonstration like that," I pointed out.

"But I want you," Susan said warmly. "You were kind to me as a child. And you had your own way of verifying my results."

"How did you know about Betsy?" I asked, the disquiet I'd felt in my room coming back a little stronger.

"Research," Susan said with a grin. I didn't like the glint in her eyes. "Your camera—Betsy did you call her? She's unique, you know."

I hadn't, actually. But I nodded as if I had and asked, "So you talked with the Fixer who made her?"

Susan gave me that maniacal grin again. "Better. I have the notes from Mr. Potter."

Mr. Potter had been an investment banker who'd tried to get rid of me by sending me to Hell. Instead, I'd haunted him to death. "He had notes on Betsy?"

"Yes, he did. He'd also speculated that she had a soul of her own, accidently captured while your Fixer fumbled about between worlds."

I looked down at Betsy, who'd always seemed so warm to me. She glowed a soft red, brighter than anything else I could see with my grayed out ghost vision. "A soul? Like a ghost?"

Susan shrugged. "I'm not sure what I'll find."

I frowned. Since when had I agreed to any sort of experiments on Betsy?

"If you'll leave her to me, that is," Susan said, gesturing to the portal. "When you pass Beyond."

It struck me that I could now pass, go to that city. I hated the idea of Betsy strapped to a table and taken apart though. "If I leave her to you, no dissection," I said.

Susan looked disturbed. "I wouldn't do that to her! She's too alive. No, I'd use her in my work. Maybe fine tune her a bit —expand her spectral abilities."

"All right," I said slowly, nodding.

"So you'll go through?" Susan asked, turning eagerly back to her console.

"I need to get my affairs in order," I told her.

Susan sighed, but agreed. "Just remember, you can't share this with any other ghosts. I just–I need my backers to see it first."

I agreed easily enough, never intending to keep the promise. Susan's work was too important, and I had to show Toni that Beppe was okay.

We left the basement and the empty mansion, driving back to the city. The twinkling lights seemed a poor imitation to the welcome I knew was waiting for me in *my* city, the one I'd be finally able to go to. Relief kept washing through me. I was finally through with this place, this land, this life or afterlife.

I was going *home*.

I STARED AT THE CLOSED SIGN, DONE IN A SPRAWLING, fancy script. Why was *The Haunting Hour*, the art gallery Toni Hermano owned, not open? It was just before midnight—normal operating hours for them.

I walked back into the dark street, wishing as always that I had some way of adjusting my collar or my cuffs. I would be leaving the next day. I'd really wanted to be able to say goodbye to Toni. I did the best I could by running my fingers along the strap of Betsy still hanging around my neck.

"Andrew! *Paisano*!" I heard Toni's voice call from behind me. I looked around, but she wasn't coming from the gallery.

She came walking down the street and I took a moment to admire her. She looked gorgeous as always, a low cut dress that showed off her cleavage as well as her curves with high heels that may as well have been ballet slippers given her graceful walk.

"I didn't know you celebrated," Toni exclaimed, handing me a tall, Fixed candle then directing the flame from her own lit taper to mine. The fire danced under her fingers, licking at them then leering hungrily towards me before settling down. Flames responded to all ghosts: arson investigators now put the undead at the top of the list for all unexplained fires.

"Celebrated?" I asked dazed as I followed her up the street. Only then did I notice the half dozen ghosts trailing behind her, also holding lit candles.

"The solstice," Toni explained.

"Oh," was all I could think to say. I hadn't known ghosts celebrated anything during the holidays. "Where are we going?" I asked after Toni greeted another ghost and pressed her into the service as well, wondering just how widespread this celebration actually was.

"To Beaker's Yard," Toni said, as if it should be obvious.

My blank look gave me away. I was never going to impress Toni with anything at this rate.

"When the veils shredded they discovered a private family burial at the Beaker house," she explained.

"Nice euphemism," I muttered as Toni turned away again. When I'd been alive the Beaker case had been a tough one that consumed more than one of the homicide detectives. I'd been in vice, so I only heard grumbling about the case after hours in the bar. The family had disappeared one by one, taken from all over the city. No one could prove anything, though, because the bodies had never turned up. Portals had sprung up near where they'd been buried, which turned out to be the backyard of one of the apartment houses they owned.

"It's the closest graveyard," Toni said, ignoring me. "I prefer these intimate gatherings to the big ceremonies, yes?"

Numbly I nodded as Toni recruited yet another ghost on the street, wondering how intimate she meant when there now appeared to be a dozen ghosts, each lit by our own internal glow that out shone the candles we carried.

We turned off the main drag, walking out of the business district and into the surrounding neighborhood. About a block away was a community pea-patch garden. A collection of the living stood outside the gate, also holding candles. They watched silently as the ghostly parade marched past, through the garden and into the courtyard of an old brick building.

Instantly the portals sprang up, each showing our individual Hells. I tried not to look at Toni's—I only caught a glimpse of waiting monsters—before I drew close enough that the appearance shifted to my own boiling clouds of nothingness with flames that would burn my soul.

A well-dressed younger man, one of the Beakers, I assumed, waited for us. He wore a bespoke suit with a cut so classic it would always look good. He directed us into a larger circle, hands waving like a magician's, fascinating and agile. His face had long features; an elongated nose and chin and almost pointed ears sticking through ginger hair.

"That's Simon," Toni whispered to me as we found our places.

Before I could ask more, Simon began. "Tonight is the longest night." His voice carried more power than I was used to hearing from a ghost, as well as a passion that had abandoned most of the dead. "A symbol of our continued existence."

I wondered if he'd been a lawyer.

"We mourn the Heaven we were promised, that we no longer believe in."

A strange happiness blossomed in my chest. I wasn't in mourning like they were, not anymore. I'd seen my Heaven again—not just promised but delivered to me on a silver plate by my family.

I smiled at Toni who frowned at me. I realized that this was supposed to be a solemn occasion and schooled my expression into something more suitable, pressing down on the budding, alien elation I felt.

"We no longer face the day with joy, the ringing of Hell's Bells brought with the dawn. But I urge you to see hope with the growing light."

A muttered sigh went through the ghostly community, otherworldly enough that I shivered. I noticed that only two of the living had followed us into the enclosed space. One wasn't affected by the noise. The other reached up and tweaked something behind her ears.

I remembered Susan hadn't seemed bothered by any of my ghostly exhalations. Did she wear these as well? Some sort of earplug or aid that filtered out ghostly subsonics? She had read Mr. Potter's notes. She knew I was capable of terrible haunting. Was it merely a matter of being comfortable? Or was it protection against me in case I turned on her?

And why would I turn on her, unless what she'd shown me was a trick?

I looked at the other mourners, suddenly no longer so smug.

We didn't sing together, and we couldn't hold hands or hug. We had to wave out our candles since we didn't have any breath to blow them out. Only a vigorous shake would put them out, as the flames were too attracted to ghosts. We stood in the dark, glowing with our own deadly pallor, the flickering portals to Hell shining behind us.

Toni thanked Simon as we walked past, depositing candles in the box he held. "So, *paisano*, tell me what you wanted," Toni said as we separated from the others.

"You don't believe it was just to see you?" I asked, finding my smile returning.

"You? You are all business," Toni said. She shrugged one shoulder. "It's a cliché, but you need to learn to live a little."

I glanced down at my ghostly form then looked back up at her, one eyebrow cocked.

"You know what I mean," she said exasperated.

"I, uhm, yeah." I paused. If I'd been alive I would have swallowed around a lump in my throat, or wiped suddenly sweating palms across my thighs. It was much harder to speak my plans aloud than I'd expected. "I may not have to," I finally told her.

Toni grew very still. "You've decided to pass Beyond?"

I merely nodded.

"Andrew! Why would you give up that way?" Frustrated, Toni slapped her hand across my shoulder, passing *through* me. It was distinctly disturbing, first to have a part of my body suddenly displaced that way and second by the chill of being that intimate with another ghost.

"What did you do that for?" I asked, betrayed and stunned.

"Because you're being an idiot." Toni glowered at me.

"It's not like that," I assured her. I looked up and down the street, and though it was quiet enough, there were still too many people and ghosts milling around given Susan's warnings of secrecy. "I can explain," I told Toni. "Not here. Someplace private, where we can talk."

"*Paisano*," Toni said flirtatiously. "If you weren't—you—I'd be flattered."

"Come on," I growled at her.

She smiled and shook her head but followed along.

I could only hope that she'd follow me into the Beyond as well.

WE ENDED UP AT MY OFFICE. THERE WERE SEVERAL THINGS I needed to take care of there, anyway. I hadn't decided what I was going to do with my files, if I should burn them or give them to my lawyer or something else. I wanted to ensure their confidentiality. I also didn't know what to do with all the natural artifacts—the rocks, pieces of glass, marbles and plastic toys—which covered the shelves of the cinder block-and-board bookcase that ran along the one wall. Each of them held a spark of *something*: life, Heaven, energy, I didn't know, that took them far enough out of the mundane world that ghosts could touch them.

Toni didn't believe me at first. I purposefully didn't tell her of Beppe. I wanted to surprise her, just show her the picture and prove that her brother had gone to Heaven. "There is no scientific explanation of Hell," she told me. "No atoms or physics."

"I have proof." I put Betsy between us and scrolled to the pictures, showing Toni the beast, then the first shot of the portal.

The dark picture of my Hell started Toni. "Oh, *paisano*," she muttered. I think she would have patted my hand if ghosts could touch.

"It gets better," I assured her. I scrolled to the next photo, expecting Beppe's Heaven.

My Hell remained.

"But I thought—wait." I thumbed through the rest of the shots.

The ones with the screen were especially telling. Betsy had captured it beautifully: the false image of my Heaven, partially covering the real image of Hell that lay behind it.

"Andrew. I'm sorry," Toni said softly. "It looks so beautiful."

I nodded, stunned. I should have known it was too good to be true, that Susan had been lying.

She was family, after all.

"Why did the picture change?" I wondered out loud.

Toni shrugged. "Maybe Susan's machine can affect things on some quantum level. Or maybe *she* is trying to protect you," Toni said, pointing to Betsy.

"How did you know—"

"You know she sometimes looks like she's alive, no? Like the living?"

I shook my head, cradling Betsy in my hands. "Her name's Betsy," I told Toni, introducing them.

Toni looked at Betsy, then up at my face. "You take good care of her," Toni said with a smile. "You can trust her." Then Toni grew more serious. "You must destroy this machine, *paisano*. Before she fools others."

I shook my head. "I can't haunt Susan." I explained my theory about the earpieces. "And the machine isn't Fixed, not really. I can't touch it."

Toni reached up to her chest, pulled her lighter out from between her breasts, and then slid it to me across the desk. "She hid your flames of Hell from you, no? Maybe you should show her real fire."

I DID MY OWN RESEARCH THEN, THE CHECKING I SHOULD have done before I'd blithely gone off with Susan. I looked up my grandnephew Bill, dead now though not a ghost if the records were to be believed. Susan was his daughter, the pictures proved it, and so we actually were related. She'd been sick as a child, something I hadn't recalled, but there were a lot of things from that time that were hazy at best.

I cursed when I discovered the company Susan worked for, who her backers were. A faith-based organization called "Going Home" that was dedicated to convincing ghosts to travel Beyond.

Was Susan's machine yet another ploy, to show a ghost Heaven so they'll willingly go into Hell?

I went back to Susan's records. Something nagged at me, an old police instinct.

Susan's medical records were online, like everyone's. The program I used to hack into them was strictly illegal and as far as I knew, only available to ghosts. The evidence was clear in retrospect. Susan hadn't really been sick, just clumsy as a child.

Too clumsy.

The break in her arm when she'd been four was a spiral fracture: that only came from twisting, not falling. The broken toes came from an object that was too heavy for a five year old to lift, let alone knock over.

Maybe I had been kind to Susan as a child, as she'd claimed. But I hadn't seen, or been kind enough.

On a whim, I did a casual search for Betsy. Sly pictures of her showed up on a web site dedicated to special artifacts, candid photos of her bright red case in my ghostly hands. I had no idea that anyone else knew about her or even had any interest.

I'd always felt she had a warmth to her—now I learned that other people thought the same. She didn't have a fan page like some of the other artifacts, for which I was both grateful and disgruntled. I knew she was special enough to merit one.

I wasted some time scrolling through websites, looking at other artifacts. There was a statue of Buddha in Thailand that seemed to have a life of its own, as chilling to the touch as a ghost but warm enough to heat a spectralgraph, a clock in Germany running with its own life force, and a drinking flagon in Wales that was merry.

Eventually I came back to my own problem and the page with Betsy. Maybe Susan wanted to get some type of revenge on me. Maybe she'd been counting on my continued distraction, or my inability to see what was right in front of me.

Or maybe there was something else she'd wanted all along.

I COULDN'T CONFRONT SUSAN WHEN SHE PICKED ME UP that evening. I needed to get out to her place, and the bus wasn't going to cut it. Instead, I asked her about Betsy. "You said you'd read Mr. Potter's notes?" They'd been missing from the artifacts website. Instead, the article was full of guesses about Betsy's true nature, some startling accurate like her spectralgraphic abilities, and some far from the truth, about how she'd jump in my hands to warn me of danger. "What did Mr. Potter say about Betsy?"

"He didn't have time to fully inspect her," Susan said. She casually rubbed her ear. I saw now that she wore something in the canal there. "You've see the website, right?"

"Found it this afternoon," I confessed. I wanted Susan to continue to underestimate me so it was easy to admit the truth.

"Ah." Susan gave me an indulgent smile. "I couldn't ask Mr. Potter about her. He died of internal hemorrhaging sometime after you'd chased him into the street and he was hit by a bus."

"Haunted him," I corrected. I'd been locked in the basement at the time, facing my own inevitable Hell. I hadn't known his final fate, though. I hadn't bothered looking it up. Though ghosts could be vengeful, we weren't passionate, not a lot of follow through.

"Okay." Susan clearly didn't understand the difference. "However, I suspect, given some of the early comments on the page by someone who called themselves The Magician, that he'd been interested in Betsy for quite some time."

I thought back to the elaborate game Mr. Potter and Mr. A— had played. Had the hiding and passing of the Disruption stone been a smokescreen to hide their attempt to acquire Betsy? "He did have quite a collection of artifacts," I mused.

"Supposedly he had a Disruption stone," Susan said, not as slyly as she'd hoped.

"Couldn't say," I told her as blandly as I could.

"Most of his artifacts went to private collectors." She sighed. "But I did get to see some of his notes on making the Disruption stones. Some of the alloys he used make up PETER."

"Pure myth," I told her, shaking my head and hoping to hide my lie.

Susan gave me a grin. "That's what most people would say about a camera with a soul."

I'd thought about Betsy for a large part of the day. If I took her apart would she be free? Did she want to be free? Or did she have her own brand of Hell waiting for her in the Beyond?

I had no answer, and no way to find out. I was determined, however, that if I ever did find a portal to Heaven that I would hold onto her as tightly as I could as I passed and hopefully give her a better place as well.

"No experiments though, right?" I said, covering Betsy with a protective hand.

"No dissection. I promise."

I didn't comment on the change of words. Susan would keep Betsy whole. But I doubted she would cherish her as I did.

TWINKLING FAIRY LIGHTS OUTLINED THE FRONT HEDGE, spotlighting even more hidden creatures. "Why would people do that?" I asked, genuinely disturbed by the half-lit vampire bats and evil pixies.

"They probably thought it would keep your kind out," Susan said.

It was good that Susan had her back turned to me so she didn't see the look I'd shot her.

Your kind. I could see the capital letters Susan had unconsciously used, all the ramifications of her belief, her mistrust and fear.

I paid more attention to the living room this time, not allowing myself to be distracted by the deliberate hum of the beast in the basement.

The room wasn't *Sealed* and inaccessible to the undead, which I found surprising given the work Susan was doing on

My Kind. When I looked more closely at the wall under the great front window I saw a curling line of chalk. During the day it had been as invisible as a ghost was in bright sunlight. Now, at night, it had its own ghostly glow.

I didn't recognize the text—some kind of Sanskrit—but I could easily guess the intent. A hidden sealing that most ghosts wouldn't see or feel.

I didn't comment on it, or point out to Susan how the letters now glowed. When we moved away from the living room I saw that they outlined a single clear path. The stairs going up were blocked by them, as were the other rooms. Any ghost would be hemmed into following only this trail.

Susan went directly to her console and the beast shuddered to life. I tracked the electrical lines, memorizing their positions. The ceiling held a smoke detector, no sprinklers, nothing to put out a fire.

I didn't want to kill Susan, to condemn her to any kind of Hell. Maybe her belief that she was doing good would save her and she'd find Heaven when she died. It was rare for a ghost to actually murder someone. We *knew* what was Beyond.

"Are you ready?" Susan asked. Her eyes gleamed with excitement. She had her own cameras set up to record the event, her proof for her sponsors. "Ready for Heaven?"

"You know that's not where I'm going," I growled at her. Now that the beast was running, drawing more power, it would be easier to kill, and I could drop this game.

Susan winced and adjusted her earpieces. "Yes, you are. You saw it yourself."

"Lies," I told her, barring my teeth. "Smoke and mirrors."

She looked away, unable to face the death's head mask I now wore. "No! It's Heaven! I showed you your Heaven!"

I let my face fall back to its usual sate.

Susan believed what she'd shown me was the truth.

"It's Hell behind that screen," I assured her.

"No, no, no," Susan muttered, turning back to her console,

making a few adjustments, desperate gestures. "It's Heaven. I made all the modifications my backers asked for. I know I have it right this time. I know it's Heaven."

"It isn't real." Maybe Susan had duped herself into believing her machine.

"But Betsy!" Susan exclaimed. "She showed you—"

"No." I motioned Susan closer. Her eyes shown with mad despair.

I hated true believers.

She gasped at the pictures. "But—how—" Susan muttered to herself about quantum states and proximity. "Look, let me show you."

Without warning Susan dashed away, and suddenly my Heaven filled the mesh screen half covering the portal again. My city shone under clear skies and brilliant stars, lit with ten thousand warm lights and hearts. I gave a deep groan. The picture wavered but held on.

"Look," I said. I took a picture with Betsy and showed it to Susan while backing away toward the stairs.

The captured image changed as if it were animated, the fog boiling away to black clouds and leaping flames.

"Just give me some more time," Susan begged. "If I can find your Hell I can reach your Heaven."

"There is no scientific construct for either," I told her. "You've tapped into my vision of the place, not the place itself."

"Then where to do the artifacts go?" Susan countered.

"Somewhere in between," I told her. Maybe like the place Betsy had been.

From the quick guilty look that crossed Susan's face I knew her sponsors had told her that too. "Let it go, Susan. Find some other way to help my kind, if that's what you really want to do."

"No, give me another year. Please. Promise me you'll come back here next Christmas, and we'll try—"

"I don't want to do this again," I told her sternly, gesturing toward the fading vision of my eternal city.

"Please, you must," Susan begged.

A holiday tradition of seeing the Heaven my life had denied while still unable to go there myself? Like the familial good will promised by the season only to be replaced with the reality of the drunken aunt, the abusive nephew, the unending sibling rivalry?

"No." I shuddered. "You need to stop this. There is no hope."

Susan shook her head. "There's always hope."

"Hope is for the living, not the dead."

Susan's eyes widened. "That's not true."

"Shut it down, Susan. Now." Maybe because I was so close to her the ghostly subsonics got through and she shivered, growing very pale. But she looked stubbornly at me, her arms crossed over her chest. "You won't stop, will you?"

Susan shook her head. "I can't," she said honestly. The gleam in her eyes shone bright and true, her obsession and madness clear.

"Then I'll have to shut it down for you."

"How?" she asked, curious and clearly not threatened.

"Doesn't matter. Just know that I can," I told her. Ghosts didn't trust the living, never had. I wasn't about to give away all our secrets. She would be gone by the time I started working with the fire.

"Give me until dawn. My notes—"

"Now, Susan." I drew closer to her slipping on the death's head mask again. I rounded on her so her back was to the stairs. "Run. While you still can."

"But—"

"Run," I growled, putting all the haunting menace I could into the single word.

I waited while she turned, hesitatingly, then finally walked back up the stairs. I growled one more warning before I went over to the console. She'd mentioned notes. A supply of notebooks, the old fashioned paper bound ones, lay in neat stacks on her desk.

I took Toni's lighter out of my pocket. Funny how the little bic's, any kind of fire starter, really, needed so little Fixing for a ghost to use.

The fire blossomed under my fingers and the paper caught easily. Though I couldn't touch the flame—could barely feel it, actually—I could still direct it along singing electrical wires and vulnerable wooden sheeting.

The beast sparked at the first touch of the flame, its strange blue aura flaring orange before subsiding. The fire burned more quickly now.

I knew the Hell flames from the portal couldn't reach out and kiss their earthly cousin, but it looked that way as the portal exploded. I instinctively protected myself by going *down*, into the earth, traveling as only a ghost can through the muddy clay. I rose just past the building then joined Susan standing in the wide circular driveway, her arms wrapped over her chest, hugging herself. She looked much more pale than I remembered but before I could ask a loud *whump* came from the house and a belch of smoke seeped out the front window. The smoke detectors wailed loud enough to be heard out here.

"I saw my Heaven, once," Susan murmured.

The smoke highlighted the fairy lights, making them look mystical and not as cheap.

"I'd expected it to be like yours, or a laboratory, someplace I could work. It was a beach, instead. All I can do right now is yearn for those empty, carefree days."

More muffled explosions came from the house, and it shivered on its foundations.

"You could go to the beach now," I said as we both took a step back.

"What's the point?" Susan asked, trembling. "The machine showed me my Hell." She looked at me with her pale ghost eyes, the madness much more apparent now.

"I'm sorry," I said. I truly was. I should have realized she wouldn't have left. "I didn't intend for this."

"I know. I did."

"What? Why? You still had hope," I told her, bewildered.

Susan shook her head. If she'd still been alive her laughter would have been bitter and cruel. "My dad took away my hope when I was too young to know better. This was just smoke and mirrors. Like everything else. Like family and holidays."

I wished I could have argued with her, but I couldn't.

"What will you do now?" I asked as flames kicked up behind the fancy windows, fueled by the scripts that had been drawn there.

The second leading cause of fire now: protection against ghosts.

"I haven't decided yet," Susan said. She leaned away from me and pointed. Now I saw the portal, a real one, which stood just inside the front door.

I didn't want to ask her which she'd seen more recently, her Heaven or her Hell. I hoped it was her beach. Either way, given the way her eyes seemed to spin on their own, I wasn't optimistic. Even if it was Heaven, she might be too insane to go.

"I'll leave you in peace to decide," I told her. To step Beyond, even to Heaven, wasn't always an easy thing.

"Thank you," Susan said gravely.

I left her behind, contemplating her fate, promising myself that I'd try to care, this time. I would see if she was still around in a year's time, maybe invite her to the Solstice gathering.

It would be the holidays after all, and Susan was truly family now.

HIGH STAKES HELL

TONI HAD BEEN RIGHT. EVEN THOUGH I WAS DEAD, merely a ghost, I still had to live a little.

When Simon Beaker, one of the murdered Beaker family, asked me to join their semi-monthly poker game, I accepted. I was certain he didn't do it out of the goodness of his heart, but rather, because Toni had asked him, bribed him, or threatened him.

Or, knowing Toni, if he'd been hesitant, some combination of all three.

Playing games of chance with the dead was very different than with the living. We didn't feel passion like they did. A straight flush, aces high, wouldn't cause our hearts to beat faster: we didn't have hearts. Same with four of a kind or a full house: no breath to catch, no sweaty palms, no bodies that betrayed us.

That didn't mean ghosts didn't have tells. We did. They were just much more subtle, like a tightening of the muscles around the eyes, or the slight curling of one hand.

Host for the game rotated between the players. I'd taken a turn already, renting the conference rooms at the big Starbucks on Capitol Hill. The gathering had felt small and intimate, the room paneled in warm wood. It had been a good night.

Tonight, Simon was hosting. He'd arranged for us to have the back room of Libby's bar, behind the mirrored doors. The room itself was quiet enough, sequestered away from the boisterous bar patrons. Black and white photos of ancient Hollywood glamour stars covered the walls, old ghosts who stared at the modern version. We only took up the back half of the room while the empty chairs and other tables sat mocking us from the other side.

The pay-in was equivalent to a very expensive dinner, complete with wine: a little rich for my tastes, but I'd done well enough at the table every time before this that I had confidence I'd make it back.

Of course, I should have known my luck was about to change.

The night started well enough. I took the pot a couple of times, while Bill, Paul, and Simon's good buddy Jose kept trading folds.

Drinks from the bar showed up halfway through the night. It wasn't that we could actually drink anything, but as a prop, it felt right. Comfortable. The staff used air-ice for our drinks, the stuff that looked like ice, kept liquids cool, but didn't actually melt. It made a sound that was particularly soothing to ghosts. More than one joke had been made about how it rattled like bones.

When the bad hands started showing up, I folded easily at first. Then I was tempted by almost good cards, betting on a hand I should have thrown away two rounds before I did.

I didn't think anything of it. Bill and Paul had been losing steadily all night. We groused together about our luck.

Finally, I'd had enough. I'd lost significantly more than my buy-in, and I knew it was time to leave. Just as I was starting to stand, Simon caught my eye.

"One last hand."

I looked at the few chips still in front of me. "I'm tapped out."

"So we don't play for money."

I didn't trust his smile. "I'm sure I don't have anything you want."

"You have your camera," Simon said casually.

"No." I stood all the way up. I would never, ever gamble Betsy away. She was the one touchstone I had to this world. She always appeared a warm red in the grayed out world of ghosts. She had her own soul, I was certain of it.

Interestingly enough, Jose also stood. I wasn't sure what he could do to me. As a ghost, he couldn't touch me. While ghosts could haunt the living, all he could do was make me uncomfortable if he started moaning, not drive me insane.

"No, not, not like that," Simon assured me with that same used-car salesman smile. "Just one use of her. I want to take some pictures with her. That's all."

"Why not just ask?"

"What's the fun in that?" Simon responded with an easy grin. He was a weird ghost. His passion was as constant as the Seattle rain, more mist than downpour, but nearly always there. He wore a bespoke suit, as fancy as any lawyer. "Besides, you might have said no."

"I could still say no."

"But now you're curious.

Damn him. He was right.

"Are you finished with your drama?" Bill asked. "Or can we get back to the game?"

"Sorry. Just Andy and me for one hand," Simon said. "If you'd like to deal though. . ."

"What if you lose?" I asked.

"Future favor," Simon offered. "Anything you ask."

Ghosts often bargained favors. It was a common enough currency. Simon was a powerful ghost, with a lot of cachet in the ghost community. A favor from him meant a lot more than a favor from me, essentially an outsider.

"Deal," I told him, sitting back down. Jose sat as well.

Of course I lost. I watched the cards carefully, but maybe Bill was in on it too. Maybe he cheated, dealt underhanded without me seeing it.

It didn't matter. I was too curious to win.

WE MET THE NEXT AFTERNOON IT DAWNED GRAY. MIST hung heavy in the air next to the sound and clouds covered the sun. If I'd been alive I would have put on a heavier coat, or even a scarf. And I wanted to. As a ghost I didn't feel the cold, but everything looked slick and chilled enough that I felt like I should.

The habits of the living died hard.

Simon was late, of course. He came with Jose, who stood behind him with his arms crossed over his chest, stretching the seams of his cheap suit to the limits, the typical position of a bodyguard. I still was unsure what Jose could do to someone like me. Then again, maybe he wasn't guarding against ghosts, but the living. Maybe Jose could be extra loud if he decided to haunt someone.

I had Betsy with me, as stipulated, slung around my neck, my hands resting on her warm case. I took a photo of the pair of them as they walked up, without focusing or bringing her up, as stealthily as I could.

For once my luck held, and neither of them noticed.

I instructed Simon on the operation of Betsy, how to set the f-stop and aperture. He barely listened, his eyes focused on her.

A sure tell.

I ended by putting her strap around Simon's neck as I handed him the camera.

"I'd never drop her," Simon assured me, eyes wide and strangely honest.

I believed him. "I know you'd never do it on purpose. This is just to prevent accidents."

Simon nodded. He let go of Betsy for a moment to pull on a strange pair of black leather gloves. They looked like racing gloves, with no fingertips, and stripes of holes down the back. They'd obviously been Fixed, though I'd never seen clothing that had been made into an artifact before.

I had a bad feeling about them, but there was nothing I could do.

Simon very carefully picked Betsy back up and focused her out across the water before he snapped the first picture. He looked at it in the viewfinder, not bothering to show Jose or myself. He nodded, satisfied, before he took another.

It was probably just my imagination, but Betsy looked pale in Simon's hands. Maybe it was the black of the gloves wrapped around her.

Simon took a couple dozen pictures in all and then deleted them. I only found out about the latter after he'd handed her back.

"I had some personal pictures there!" I complained.

"Sorry." Simon didn't look sorry at all.

I stayed on the pier after Simon and Jose left. Betsy warmed slowly in my hands. I blamed the chill of the day. I took a few photos myself, searching for meaning in the open water, the far islands, the patterns of the birds, the waves.

Nothing made any sense to me.

I deleted the photos from Betsy before I left. I didn't need to email them to myself.

I'd only bothered explaining how the camera lens worked to Simon. He hadn't asked, and I certainly hadn't mentioned, that Betsy could be set to instantly email every picture she took.

I felt certain that if Betsy could talk, she wouldn't have told him either.

———

THOUGH I RESENTED SPENDING THE MONEY, I STILL PAID

for all the photos to be printed, as well as having a special sigil drawn on the back of each so that they were Fixed and I could handle them. I took them back to my office, locking the door against any intruders. I didn't necessarily feel safe there, though there were plenty of people and ghosts in the other offices. I just felt the need not to be alone after standing so long on that pier.

The candid of Jose and Simon had a weird glow, as if what they carried had extra spectral weight. Plus, the light was a ghastly green, the same awful light that Hollywood often used to portray alien guts and blood.

The other pictures started out normal, just the sound, the flat water, the clouded sky and the distant land. Then extra mists began to blur the edges, unwelcome fingers across the scene. They left me feeling lonely and cold, alone at the edge of the world.

Then the pictures changed. It was as if Simon had started to move while snapping photos, too quickly for Betsy to focus. However, I remembered him standing stock still. The images blurred, and one had strange, warm red lights casting erratic trails across the sky.

The last three photos baffled me at first. Mists now filled the image, billowing menacingly. They reminded me of the clouds of Hell I always saw when I looked through a Portal to the Beyond.

I thought I saw images hidden in the fog, vague, nightmarish shapes. I got out my magnifying glass, scrutinizing the pictures. Maybe I was imagining things, but I thought I saw something there. Something not human. It was as if Simon had taken a photo beyond a different veil, peering into one of the half dimensions that modern physicists now explored.

But how? How had he made Betsy take those pictures? How had he peeked through that mist? And what did he intend to do with the monsters he found there?

I had more questions than answers. At least I had a place to start. I gathered the photos and headed down to the bus station.

It was going to be a very long trek from the city to the outskirts of Redmond. However, that's where I'd find Susan, my grandniece, haunting the remains of her burned down laboratory. She'd been an atomic physicist when she'd been alive, and an expert on veils and those dimensions.

I just hoped she'd be sane enough tonight to help me.

I FINALLY MADE IT TO SUSAN'S PLACE JUST PAST THE witching hour. I'd visited her a few times since she'd become a ghost. The first occasion had been at the request of the Defender's office, the group of ghosts who'd been lawyers when they'd been alive and now ensured the rights of the dead with more zeal than was natural. Susan had started haunting her neighbors, shrieking and howling through the night. Because she was insane, no one had been able to reason with her.

There wasn't a way to kill a ghost, to force them to step through a Portal into the Beyond. However, you could always Banish them, disassemble their ectoplasm temporarily. The ghost would reincorporate wherever their bones were, which in Susan's case, was the Redmond cemetery, out at Cedar Lawns. They'd tried that a couple of time to no avail.

I'd been able to get through to Susan and she'd stopped her yowling, sticking to her own house. Luckily, the Defender's office was able to buy the property so Susan didn't have to leave. There was no concern about a human or vandal squatting there: Susan would haunt anyone or anything to death that tried to hang out.

Only a fool would approach a ghost in their lair, and in Susan's case, only the suicidal.

Still, Susan was family, and she tended to take one or two steps closer to sane when I came to visit.

That night, Susan paced around the circular driveway to what had once been a rambling mansion. The fountain in the center had long ago filled with leaves. On a whim, I'd taken pictures of it once. Sparkling water shot out of the top of it, and it glistened with spectral light, looking fresh and new. I didn't know how or why Susan could have that effect. I wondered if it was part of her madness, never seeing a single thing, but always a double vision, of what had once been layered on top of what was there today.

The house had fallen more in on itself, a great, gaping hole where the roof had been. Boarded windows stared out blankly. The evil fairies and zombie gnomes guarding the front glittered with their own light, as if they'd also been turned into ghosts.

Susan didn't acknowledge my presence when I walked up the driveway, so I just joined her, marching in circles. She muttered equations and numbers as she walked, trying to solve the unsolvable.

Eventually Susan's pace slowed. She started repeating the alphabet with commentary. "G, G is much more important than A," she murmured. "And seven, seven is prime, like one and A."

"What about S?" I asked, trying to get her to see me.

Susan looked at me for the first time, madness still whirling in her eyes. "There is no S," she told me primly. "Not if I'm going to get the equations right this time. For the Portal. So I can step Beyond."

I knew better than to mention the Portal that stood just beyond the closed door of the house. Susan refused to believe it was real. She claimed that it only sometimes showed Heaven, and the rest of the time it showed Hell. I'd never seen it do such a thing myself, but I suspected if it was possible to change your fate, Susan could.

"I'm sure you'll finish it soon," I told her. "In the meanwhile, do you want to see your competition's work?"

Susan leveled a direct glare at me. "No one's at my level. No one's even been able to duplicate my work."

That wasn't an idle claim. As far as I could tell, no one had been able to rebuild Susan's beast. Her notes on it had been destroyed in the fire, and Susan didn't share well with anyone.

"Then maybe you could tell me about these," I said, showing her the photos of the mist.

"Betsy?" Susan asked. She caressed the picture with a finger.

I winced at the longing in her voice. Susan had also lusted after my camera. I hadn't brought Betsy with me this time. I needed Susan to answer my questions. When I brought Betsy, Susan spent the entire visit talking with my camera instead of me. It was also very disturbing when I left such a visit. Ghosts don't have tear ducts. They can't cry. But with Susan, it was a near thing.

"I'll bring her next time," I promised. So far I'd been pretty good remembering Susan and coming to see her. I suppose it was because she was family, in more than one sense.

Susan flipped through the pictures, stopping at the first smeared one. "Interesting," she murmured. She flipped to the next one. "Fascinating."

"What do you see?"

Susan didn't answer, just looked through the rest of the photos, comparing the first and last, then really studying the last one for a long while.

I waited as patiently as I could. Susan obviously saw something I didn't.

"In 2012 the veils between the Seen and Unseen worlds were shredded," she started in a lecturing tone.

I nodded and didn't roll my eyes, though that was old history.

"This brought verification of other worlds and veils as well. The two primary unknowns that the scientific community has never been able to answer are, why did the veils shred, and why did only those particular veils shred?

Susan looked up at me. I'd never seen her so sane as a ghost. "The existence of Heaven and Hell do not prove the existence of higher beings, such as God or Satan, though the corollary is strong. Supposition that God only let through what humanity could handle is often stipulated. Others believe that the Devil won a round, which is why the veils were destroyed."

I nodded. I'd heard all those arguments as well, not necessarily from scientists.

After a brief pause of studying the last photo again, Susan continued. "Some of the other veils hide creatures much worse than us." She traced the shape of something monstrous in the mists of the picture, outlining it with a ghostly glow.

"These veils cannot be shredded," Susan instructed me, pointing at the photo. "The first shredding just ended the world as people knew it. These would end the world." She paused, looking off in the distance.

"Go on," I prompted her.

"I don't have proof that every peek beyond the curtain weakens it. But I will when I finish my work. It's how we might be able to move all the ghosts Beyond and into Heaven."

I wasn't touching that one with a ten-foot poll.

"However, I have preliminary evidence that the veils can be weakened." Susan switched her piercing gaze back at me. "You must stop whoever is doing this."

"I'll try," I promised, chilled by more than just her burning command.

Susan flipped through the pictures again. When she looked back up at me, a death's head mask slipped over her features, disturbing even for me. "Oh, you'll do more than try. You need revenge."

"Revenge? For what?"

"Forcing an artifact through a veil hurts the object. Drains it." She pointed to the photo with the strange warm red lights streaked across the sky. "Draws the light right out of them."

Comprehension dawned slowly on me.

Simon had hurt Betsy when he'd taken these photos. It hadn't been my imagination that she'd looked gray in his hands.

I was going to kill him.

BECAUSE OF SIMON'S PASSION, HIS BESPOKE SUIT AND HIS general allocution, I'd assumed he was a lawyer. When I checked the local Defender's office, his name didn't show up on any of the ledgers.

However, it wasn't difficult to find him. His office was down near the piers, close to where we'd met for our photo op, in an old warehouse that had long ago been turned into trendy lofts and office space. Simon's office was on the second floor, facing the street, not the water.

As a ghost, I could no longer see bright colors. Simon's office was no exception, all brown, black and beige, faded and dark enough to depress even the dead. Though the door was open, no one manned the reception area. A discreet buzzer sat on one corner of the desk, with a red eye that glowed with the half light of being Fixed. I pressed it, then snatched my hand back. The sensation had been distinctly disturbing, as if my finger had passed through it. Possibly it had. I'd read about fields that measured and responded to ectoplasm. I figured this had been one of them, and not only had I announced my presence, I'd told whoever was in the back that I was a ghost as well.

While I cooled my heels I drifted over to the cabinet displaying the company's wares. Only then did I start to get an idea of what Simon, or rather his company, did.

The shelves were lined with artifacts. At first I thought they were all natural, those things that held a spark of *something*— life, Heaven, energy, I don't know what—that automatically made them usable by both the living and the dead. Every ghost collected them. I had a bookcase full of these knick-knacks in my own office, as well as a couple in my pocket.

Then I looked more closely. The artifacts practically glowed with energy. The case must have been lined with lead or charmed, because I didn't feel great power emanating from it.

More than one of the tiny things felt off to me. A creepy doll's head with sickly green glass eyes stared holes in my ectoplasmic flesh. An empty glass bottle of soda glistened with an unholy light.

All of these things had been made, not found. Or perhaps found, then twisted by Simon's company.

"What do you think of our latest line?" came Simon's silky voice from the door leading to the back rooms. He gave me his typical salesman smile as he came forward. Jose stood beside him, glaring at me. I cheerfully ignored the muscle, focusing on Simon. "You make artifacts." I figured I'd start with the obvious.

"Sometimes. Usually, though, I employ the best Fixers in Seattle and provide them with resources."

"Don't Fixers generally fix things that are useful?" I gestured toward the buzzer on the desk. "Not natural artifacts?"

"But we've found that starting with artifacts makes it easier to imbue them with further properties." Simon keyed in a code on the far side of the case. After a soft *click* the door opened.

A wave of what I could only call evil washed over me.

Simon drew out a tiny snow leopard, made out of black and white plastic. The toy was a cub, and probably had been cute before it had been Fixed. Now, it's dead blue painted eyes glared at me, and instead of a smile it gave me a deadly grin. I was loathe to touch it, afraid that it might bite me, or worse, poison me.

"So what does it do?" I asked, quelling my desire to backup and get away from the cursed thing.

Simon ran a finger down the toy's spine, as if caressing it. The wrongness radiating off it increased. "It's a protection piece. It turns away those who are—lesser than the owner." He gave me his shark's grin. "A useful toy, isn't it?"

I shook my head. "There are spells—"

"Not as effective. They need to be strengthened, from time to time."

I stopped myself from nodding. I knew he spoke the truth. I'd recently had to repower the charms that protected the file cabinet in my office.

"This little guy needs so much less."

"Just a drop or two of human blood?" I joked.

"Animal will do," Simon deadpanned, with that same predatory grin.

I didn't bother to find out if he was serious or not. I didn't really want to know. "So you have Fixers that make these things?"

Simon opened the cupboard to put the tiger cub away. The power that poured out distracted me, making me shiver. If I'd had flesh, it would have been crawling.

"Sorry?" I said when I realized Simon had answered me and I hadn't heard a word he'd said.

"It's all right. They're very distracting. Yes, my Fixers take normal artifacts and bring extra dimensions to them."

"From the other veils?" I guessed.

"Exactly!" Simon exclaimed. He peered curiously at me. "What do you know about these other dimensions?"

"Just that we shouldn't be weakening them by pulling things through them. Or pushing them through. Like Betsy."

Simon waved a negligent hand in my general direction, dismissing my accusations. "Scientists don't know that for certain. No one really does. I sincerely doubt that the work I do here would end the world."

"That's probably what Oppenheimer thought—how could splitting one little atom go wrong?"

Simon looked at me, considering. "Betsy came from beyond one of those other veils," he told me softly.

I didn't want to believe him, though I knew she was very special. She was nothing like his creatures.

"Besides," Simon continued. "What's the worst thing that could happen if more veils were shredded? If we found more of the things that go bump in the night? The living have survived us, some might even claim they're better now because of our influence."

Simon's main tell in poker was his earnest face, the one where he tried to convince us of his innocence.

He wore that same expression now. There was something wrong about bringing those creatures over, some cost he wasn't disclosing. Either that, or he didn't care what happened.

"You're crazy," I told him. "You can't control whatever comes through. You shouldn't do this."

Finally, Simon showed me his real smile, the one that was all cool condescension and superiority. He was more alien than ghost, all his humanity drained away. "You'll find I already am. Jose, it's time for Mr. Cullen to leave."

Jose was already slipping on that pair of black, fingerless, leather gloves that I'd seen Simon wear before, when he'd been handling Betsy. I expected Jose to pull out a banishment gun or some other gear to threaten me with.

Instead, Jose walked right up to me, into my personal space, and put his hand *through* me, into my chest.

The feeling of my heart being displaced was horribly disturbing. Particularly since it was a ghost doing the displacing.

Then Jose moaned. The sound traveled straight into my ectoplasm, amplified by the gloves.

I trembled with the sensation. It was similar to a banishment gun, my cells suddenly shaking apart, being torn asunder.

When I took a step back Jose followed me, moaning louder. With each step I felt my hold on the world loosen. I could also see Jose getting stronger, more defined.

Could he have destroyed me? Or would he have just banished me? I didn't wait to find out. I wrenched myself away, out the door and out of the building.

I stood panting on the sidewalk, the night surprisingly cool against my skin. I looked at my hands. They shook, but as far as I could tell I hadn't been diminished, made less that I was.

However, I had even bigger problems now. I had to shut down Simon's business, and soon, before he could diminish the whole world.

———

ALL THE OFFICERS WHO'D WORKED ON THE BEAKER murders were dead, and they'd all stepped Beyond. However, I still figured the SPD was my best place to start asking questions. Simon held a lot of power in the ghost community, but that didn't mean anything to the living.

I made an appointment with an officer who'd known me when I'd been alive. He'd been just out of the academy. Now he was facing retirement.

Ed met me in the reception area. I was the only ghost waiting in the wide-open room, avoiding the floor to ceiling windows that let in too much light and washed me out. The office was quiet: it was that lull between supper and people going out. Ed handed me a visitor's badge with a casually scribbled sigil on the back of it, powerful enough to make my fingers tingle when I touched it.

The SPD had stronger Fixers than I think anyone knew.

The bullpen sat empty, the officers gone for the night. Case files and folders surrounded the monitors and tablets on the desks: the paperless office had been promised for a century or more, and while tablets and personal devices had made a dent, paper still ruled. It was comforting actually to see the room remained stubbornly human.

"How can I help you Andy?" Ed said, indicating the visitor chair that had been placed beside his desk, the only Fixed thing in the room.

"It's probably a wild goose chase but do you know anything about the Beaker murders? It was a family that disappeared—"

"Yeah, I know," Ed said. He looked away, his lips pressed

hard together. "You know my dad was on that case, right? Ate him right up."

Only when Ed said something did I remember that I'd known his father, and that I associated *him* with the Beaker case. No wonder my subconscious had prompted me to come and talk with his son. I shook my head. "Sorry Ed, I'd forgotten. Look, just forget I asked."

"No," Ed said, looking straight at me. "Tell me. It's that bastard Simon Beaker, isn't it?"

"What do you know about Simon?" I asked warily. On the one hand, Simon was a ghost, and in many ways I felt more loyalty to him and our kind than to any officer. On the other hand, Simon was a ghoul who needed to be stopped.

"Simon was the third one to go missing. His car also went missing—the only one. All the other disappearances followed the exact same pattern. Dad always thought there was something wrong there. Plus—" Ed paused and looked around the empty room, as if verifying we were still alone. "There was a body buried with the others, and dental records said it was Simon. However, it was the only body that had been burned. Dad always wondered if someone was trying to disguise the man's face, in case he'd been dug up early."

"So you're saying Simon may not have been killed with the others?"

Ed chuckled bitterly. "Dad theorized Simon *was* the killer."

"What? That's insane," I said, trying to throw Ed off the trail. Simon was creepy and power hungry, and anyone who met him knew that. I'd met mass murderers before. They had a different feel to them, a callousness and lack of empathy that chilled all their interactions. The coldness Simon had shown me was similar, but just different enough to leave me with doubts.

Then again, dying did change a person.

"The Defense office had shot down any inquiry into the case," Ed insisted. "What does that tell you?"

It told me that the murderer was probably a ghost and still around. "That doesn't mean it was Simon," I said slowly.

"My dad chased down every lead on his own time for decades after the case went cold. He interviewed and re-interviewed every witness, retraced every step of each victim, took accounting classes at night so he could follow the money trails on his own. Millions—maybe billions—went unaccounted for during the chaos of so many family members going missing." Ed clenched his hands together, as if he was trying to contain his emotions. "My dad—my dad was a good man. Did good. Deserved Heaven. But he delayed it, fucking walked away from it, so he could go confront that bastard Simon after he'd died.

"The last time I saw him, as a ghost, before he stepped Beyond, he told me that he had proof. He'd seen Simon's Hell. It was filled with all his victims waiting for him."

"That isn't really proof," I pointed out.

"No, it isn't. And we couldn't prosecute even if it was true." Ed collapsed in on himself, as if the reality of the situation had just come crashing down on him.

"Your dad did step through, right?" I asked Ed.

"Yeah."

"Good. He did deserve Heaven. I'm glad he got it." I stood to go.

"Wait—what about Simon?"

I felt the change start, and didn't try to stop it. I let my face take on a death's head grin. "Don't worry about Simon. I'll make sure he gets what he deserves."

I WAITED UNTIL IT WAS FULLY DARK BEFORE I MADE MY WAY to *The Haunting Hour*, the art gallery owned by Toni Hermino. My motives for seeking her out were murky at best. I was seeking confirmation of Simon's true nature, but I also wanted to see her, to let someone know what I was doing, that I was confronting Simon. Not that I was delusional enough to think Toni would mourn my passing, but I still wanted someone to know, in case this turned out to be my last act.

I brought Betsy with me, loaded with special photos. I wanted to take pictures with her as well, to document the strangeness of Simon's artifacts.

The Haunting Hour, while open, was empty of customers. Toni sat, wearing a bored expression, at the back of the gallery, casually flicking through the news on her tablet. The artifact was hideously expensive: personal devices were almost impossible to Fix, as they didn't always rest in the same spot. Attaching a sigil to them didn't work either, not like it did for transportation.

Toni's expression brightened when she saw me. "*Paisano!*" she said as she stood, giving a sensual wiggle. If she'd been alive, it would have settled her dress more comfortably over her curves, a habit of the living that she didn't need as a ghost: her clothing couldn't budge from her dead body.

Its effect on others was still successful. If I'd had a heart, it would have started beating harder.

The exhibit in the gallery was focused more on the living, with bright abstracts and florals better suited for a dentist's office in my opinion. Only a few pieces were meant for our kind, with ghostly squiggles that always looked like children's finger painting to me. One piece was new, with both green and blue absurd lines. It showed no true life: such passion departed with death.

"Hey Toni," I said, walking across the scarred wooden floor to the back counter. "How goes it?"

Toni fixed me with a steady look. "You're pale," she accused. "What happened?"

"What do you know about Simon Beaker?"

The temperature in the gallery dropped several degrees due to the frosty look Toni shot me. "Simon is a good, personal friend. Very important in the community."

"What if he wasn't who he claimed to be?"

"Do you have proof?" Toni volleyed back, crossing her arms over her chest.

I shook my head.

"I thought *polizia* were only concerned with facts," she spat.

I bit my lips together, pausing for a moment. Something about Simon unsettled Toni. That alone told me just how powerful he was. "I don't know for certain," I told her gently. "I'm going to confront him tonight to find out."

"Find out what?"

I quickly told her about the last word from a dead cop, without mention Ed.

"I've heard these rumors before. They aren't true. Besides, you can't take the word of a ghost who's gone Beyond," Toni said flatly.

"No, I can't. That's why I'm going to go talk with Simon."

"What do you care?" Toni asked. "Ghost politics don't interest you. You are barely a part of the community." She paused, her eyes sweeping over me. "Ah."

I realized that my hands had instinctively dropped down to Betsy, cupping around her protectively and caressing her.

"His company makes artifacts, yes?"

I risked telling her the truth. "From beyond other veils."

Toni grew very still. "That's not good, *paisano*." She crossed herself. "Those places must remain undisturbed."

"I agree. And Susan agrees as well."

Toni nodded. "Good."

I pulled back. "Thank you, Toni. I'm sorry I had to ask, but I had to get some kind of confirmation before I went to talk with Simon. I'll let you know how it goes."

"Oh no. You are not dropping this on me then leaving. I am coming with you."

"Toni, it may be dangerous. Simon has a body guard, Jose—"

"Pfft." Toni dismissed my concern with a wave of her hand.

"Gallantry doesn't suit you. Besides, this Jose, you've tangled with him once already, yes? He's why you're looking pale?"

Grimly I nodded.

"I will deal with him. Besides, you have less life to lose than I do."

At my raised eyebrow she gave an exasperated sigh. "You know what I mean."

As Toni locked the door of the gallery behind us, I told her quietly, "I'm going to owe you another favor."

We were a few blocks away before Toni bothered to reply. "No. If what you say is true, it's the community who owes you."

Neither of us bothered acknowledging that it was actually the whole bloody world.

———

ORANGE LIGHT FROM THE STREET LAMPS BATHED THE END of the waterfront where Simon's office sat, cutting through the dark. The black pavement glistened with new rain. It all seemed so clean and sanitary, safe from the things that went bump in the night.

The door to the building was locked, and no lights shone from the second story office windows.

"Where to?" I asked Toni, assuming she had an idea where Simon might be.

Toni led me halfway across the deserted street before turning back and saying, "Take a picture."

I shrugged and did as she asked, showing her the result.

The building itself had a strange residual glow, almost as if it were Fixed. An eerie green light shone from Simon's office windows, sickly and pale.

"Now shoot there," Toni directed, pointing toward the waterfront just beyond the building.

I snapped photos on either side, a matched set, and then showed them to Toni.

"What are we looking for?" I asked as she flipped back and forth between them.

"Trails," she said, as if it were the most obvious thing in the world.

I continued to photograph more and more of the waterfront, inching away from the building in front of us, until Toni finally exclaimed, "There."

Several hundred feet away was a smudge of the same strange green light that came from Simon's windows. "This way," Toni said, leading imperiously.

I followed as only a good flunky would, photographing as we went. The light grew stronger, more blighted, in the pictures, the closer we got. We followed the trail down to the end of a commercial pier. It wasn't well lit, but it didn't need to be: as ghosts, we all carried our own light, Toni, myself, Simon and Jose.

I wasn't sure what I was going to say to Simon, how to confront him. I'd given it some thought. However, I needn't have bothered. Toni barreled right up to Simon, demanding, "Is it true?"

Simon turned. He wore the black leather gloves I'd seen him in before. A glowing marble sat in the palm of one hand.

"You shouldn't believe everything you hear," Simon said mildly. He caressed the marble with a finger. I took a photo without asking, though I didn't dare take my focus way from them long enough to look at it.

Jose materialized at my side. I nearly groaned when I saw he wore an identical set of gloves. I'd hoped they only had one pair between them. Of course, my luck wasn't that good.

"That's not an answer," Toni protested, arms akimbo staring at Simon.

"It isn't meant to be, Antonia," Simon said without looking at her.

I didn't like the way he kept talking to the thing he held in his hand, or how it grew brighter. "Life, as you know, is infinitely more complicated than that, *bella.*" Now he turned to face her. "Some secrets should stay buried, no?" he asked, deliberately mocking Toni's accent.

I didn't bother holding back my ghostly growl at his insinuations. Nor did I care. It was just us ghosts out there, no humans. We could shake the very foundations of the pier with our yowling and no one would care.

"You wouldn't," Toni declared, now holding herself, hands clinging to her bare forearms. If she'd been human, I would have seen gooseflesh all up and down her skin.

"There's very little I wouldn't dare to do, my dear."

I watched Toni crack, growing brittle under Simon's gaze. Finally she had to look away. First she stared out over the black, empty water, and then she finally turned toward me. "I'm sorry, *paisano,*" she said softly.

"Don't be," I told her. I didn't feel betrayed. She was as much a creature of circumstances as I was.

"If you don't mind, we have work to do," Simon said, all his attention turned back to the little marble.

Toni held her head high as she walked the few feet to join me, but I knew it cost her dearly.

The thing in Simon's palm blinked, sending shivers down my spine. I had to stop him. The sort of awful creature he held would tear the world apart, I knew. So I went with the next plan, hoping Toni would back me up.

"I can prove it," I told Simon, stepping forward.

"No," Toni said to me. "It's not worth the risk."

She had no idea what I meant. It didn't matter, though. She was determined to help me sell it.

"I must," I told her quietly. "I can prove those ugly rumors," I said more loudly, walking toward Simon.

"Hmph," he said, disbelievingly. "Do you have this proof with you?"

"Honestly? No. I don't have it. Yet." I rubbed the back of

my neck with my hand, as if I was embarrassed. "But I'll get it. One day."

"Why would I care about proof for something I didn't do, that you don't even have?" Simon asked, exasperated.

"Because you'll never know when you're safe, and when you're not. When I've finally gathered together all the pieces."

"What is this supposed awful deed? And your proof?"

I stepped closer, raising Betsy.

"No, Andrew," Toni said.

Though I wasn't alive, warmth still washed through me. I wasn't alone, for once.

I knew all Simon's tells. We'd played poker together for six months. He currently thought he had all the cards.

"You know she's special," I said, gesturing with Betsy. "You forced her to photograph things beyond a veil."

"And?" Simon said, miming impatience. I knew he'd started to get nervous.

"You're not the only one who knows how to do that." I quickly scrolled through the photos to the ones I'd loaded earlier, the pictures of my Hell that I'd captured with Susan's machine.

It was a gamble. I'd killed Susan's beast. I'd never be able to replicate these photos for anyone else's Hell. I was betting Simon didn't know that.

However, that bluff seemed to pay out. Simon put the pieces together quickly. He nodded. "You could publish pictures of my Hell, if these ugly rumors were true, which I am still not admitting to," he admonished, as weasily as any politician.

I nodded. "You can never be sure when you walk by a Portal if I'm there, or someone else is, recording how your victims are all waiting for you."

"Even if that is what my Hell looks like, it isn't proof," Simon maintained.

"The community's opinion doesn't need proof."

Simon studied my face for a moment before he tossed the little marble to Jose.

Toni gasped.

Jose held the marble up in front of Toni's face. She seemed mesmerized by it. His other hand had already pushed into her chest.

"If you're lying, I will kill her," Simon said from behind me. "Drain away the force and will that animates her, until she's just a gelatinous heap of ectoplasm."

One of the hardest things I've ever had to do, in either life or death, was to turn away from Toni and back toward that scum Simon. I told him, with all the honesty I could muster, "I'm not lying."

Simon studied me carefully. He knew all my bluffs as well, or at least thought he did. What he didn't realize was that I'd never tried to call the pot on less than a busted pair before. I'd always had something, some vague hope.

I'd never lied through my teeth like this.

"What do you want?" Simon finally asked. His anger told me he was close to folding.

"Let her go," I said, still not turning around, not trusting myself, what I might try to do to Jose.

I heard a quiet moan of relief from Toni. I made myself continue, not rush to her side. "Make artifacts the normal way. Stop weakening the veils."

"How will you know I'm keeping my promise? Are you and Antonia going to come and inspect my offices and warehouses every day?" Simon sneered.

"No need," I told him. I showed him the spectral image of his building. "That light? Is not normal. And will tell me everything I need to know."

Simon snorted. "This?" he said, pointing at Betsy. "Is not normal. If you took a picture of her, she'd have the same glow."

"Maybe," I said, my fingers falling into a familiar caress. I knew Betsy glowed, but it was a different kind of light. "Maybe she came from a different place. Portals lead to both Heaven and Hell. Not all the veils hide monsters. The mists might disguise angels as well."

"You don't believe that."

"Doesn't matter what I believe. What matters is that you know I'll be checking up on you. Often."

Simon nodded. Relief flooded in so profound that if I'd been alive, my knees would have been weak. Finally I turned away from him and walked back to where Toni stood, looking pale, determined and triumphant.

"I'm sorry," I told her as we headed back to street.

"Please," Toni said. "I had him just where I wanted him."

I allowed her her bravado.

"You're going to have to be very careful, Andrew," Toni warned. She ran one finger along Betsy's case. "He'll be after her now. And you."

I shrugged. I knew I'd make a great enemy that night.

As well as lost my regular poker game.

"Did you believe that? What you said? About maybe Betsy being an angel?"

"Doesn't matter," I told Toni. And it didn't. Angel or monster, Betsy was still my best girl.

POSTCARDS FROM HELL

Mrs. Lorenzo wasn't like any ghost I'd ever met.

She looked as we all did, slightly pale with her own slight glow, wearing the clothes she'd been buried in: a three-quarter sleeve hand-knit white sweater over what must have been an eye-searing tropical print dress, pearls the size of jawbreakers strung tightly around her ample neck, and cheap white sandals that wouldn't have lasted a week if she'd been living.

Because she was a ghost, none of her clothes moved or grew old. When she sat down in the guest chair in my office, her hands smoothed her skirt out of habit, not because if had climbed up.

So it wasn't her clothes that made her different. Or her looks: A Hispanic woman in her late 50s, with salt and pepper curls, hard features, stubbornly fat, and perpetually tired.

No, it was her energy, her very soul, that made her stand out.

She *cared*.

It wasn't that ghosts couldn't feel as intensely as the living. But things didn't matter like they used to, once you were dead. We tended to drift, not to drive.

Mrs. Lorenzo had never let her foot off the gas for a second.

I wondered briefly if she'd been even more assertive when she'd been alive, and this was the toned down version.

It was a horrifying thought.

"You must help me find my husband," Mrs. Lorenzo pleaded, leaning on my rickety desk. It was a good thing she was dead, because while her size was still large, her weight, now, was insubstantial. "Please! The ferrymen have him. You must rescue him!"

I leaned back as far as I could in my captain's chair, trying to get away from the emotional onslaught. The only person I'd ever seen with such intensity had been Beppe, after he'd indulged in a drug called Slide that let ghosts *feel*. It had been the most insidious stuff I'd ever experienced.

But Mrs. Lorenzo wasn't drugged. This was her natural state.

"Who are the ferrymen?" I asked. I was a private investigator, not a superhero. If he'd been kidnapped, maybe I could help, though most likely I'd turn Mrs. Lorenzo toward the police.

"Ah, you have not dealings with them, no? No. You are *gringo*, not like us." She gave a great sigh, heaving her impressive bosom. "I died here, in America. My poor Pepe—" She paused, giving another tremendous sigh. "He was visiting relatives in Mexico when he died. In Las Alamadas."

"You're certain he's a ghost?" I asked. "And that he's still—with us?" Maybe these ferrymen had tricked Mrs. Lorenzo into thinking they were bringing her husband with them.

"Yes. Yes! I have emails. Phone calls."

"Skype? Pictures?" I asked.

"We are poor people," Mrs. Lorenzo assured me. "We have no such fancy technology down in Las Alamadas. And it has taken me decades to raise the money. Decades!"

"So you're certain it's him." It would be a very, very long con, but I'd heard of such games recently.

"I know my own husband," Mrs. Lorenzo said stiffly.

Even her disapproval showed more life than most ghosts' violent arguments.

It was exhausted being in the same room with her. Particularly my small office, with just two chairs, my falling-down desk, a cabinet in the corner full of client files, and the cinder block-and-board bookcase that ran along one wall, scattered with natural artifacts: rocks, keys, broken rings, dried flowers, and other knick-knacks, each of them holding a spark of *something*: life, Heaven, energy, I didn't know what, just that they comforted me. All ghosts collected them.

"Death changes people," I cautioned her.

"Not my Pepe."

I gave my own sigh. "So you paid the ferrymen to bring his bones up here?"

"You don't know what the borders are like," Mrs. Lorenzo said with a haughty sniff. "Legitimate immigration is nearly impossible. Particularly for people like us."

"And now the ferrymen—won't give you his bones? Won't let him go? Until, what, you pay them more money?" I asked. I was surprised at the amount of incredulity I felt.

It appeared her emotional condition was contagious.

I didn't like it.

"Yes. Exactly. Just like the *coyotes*, eh? The ones who bring across the living?" Mrs. Lorenzo *tsked*. "We thought we were dealing with reputable people. The leader went to school with my cousin! There was talk of them, yes, marrying into the family. Now, this is how they treat us?"

"How are they keeping him?" I asked, really not wanting to get into her family history. Ghosts weren't without resources. I couldn't imagine the logistics holding a ghost against its will.

"The room is *Sealed*, obviously," Mrs. Lorenzo said. "But it is awful place. Awful! Only a strong man, like my Pepe, could stay there, could make such a journey."

"Why?" I asked. Then it occurred to me. "Oh."

Pepe was traveling with his bones. Which meant he also traveled with a Portal to the Beyond.

Most ghosts stayed on this earth because they knew exactly what Hell waited for them in the Beyond.

I had to assume that whatever Pepe's Hell was, it had to be worse than living with Mrs. Lorenzo.

That, also, was a horrifying thought.

Which meant that Pepe's time was rapidly running out. No ghost could resist the siren's song of a Portal for long. We were supposed to step through. It took a strong will to stay instead, no matter the Hell Beyond.

"How do they stop a ghost from getting revenge after they're freed?" I asked. Again, it didn't make sense. The very nature of being dead made us vengeful.

"That's the worse part of all," Mrs. Lorenzo said. She finally deflated, her energy fading away. She leaned closer across the desk, lowering her voice. "There are stories, rumors, of what happens when you don't pay. Of artifacts, not like these," she said dismissively, waving her hand toward my collection. "Strong. Too strong." She whispered. "Made. From human souls."

I nearly scoffed. Then I remembered Betsy, my best girl, my camera who always glowed with a warm red heart. She was an artifact made from something different, possibly a soul from Beyond a different veil: an angel, perhaps.

"These artifacts *defend* these people, these bloodsucking monsters. Please. Please! You must help me get him back."

"I'll try to find where they're keeping him," I said. I wasn't about to promise more.

""No," Mrs. Lorenzo said firmly. "You have to help me. More than that. Antonia said you were a good man. Please, Mr. Collin."

"Toni sent you?" I asked, surprised. The beautiful Antonia Hermino and I weren't dating—ghosts didn't date. But if we'd both been living, I'd probably have called her my girlfriend.

"Yes, Toni."

The silence was more disapproving than Mrs. Lorenzo's baleful stare.

"I'll help your husband escape from the ferrymen," I told Mrs. Lorenzo.

I knew I was going to regret it before I even started.

NORMALLY, TONY WOULD BE AT HER ART GALLERY *THE Haunting Hour* from when it opened at midnight until four or five. But tonight, she'd convinced me to meet her at the night market in Chinatown.

When I'd been alive, the market had taken up merely two blocks off Jackson. Now it sprawled six blocks, from Jackson to Dearborn and beyond, plus several side streets, a thriving market for both legal and semi-legal goods.

Tinkling music and the rushing sound of metal balls flowing through the Pachinko machines floated out above me. Of course, there were online versions, and even modern electronic machines, but the night market had old-fashioned, mechanical editions near the northern entrance, where a person physically shot balls into the field of needles, bouncing them into the prize corners, like pinball on steroids. There was even a Fixed machine, with its own line of lonely ghosts, trying to recapture some sort of thrill.

The living who wandered near the entrance had bags bulging with bok choy, ginger, rice, cabbage, carrots, blessing scrolls, arsenic powder for curses, and chalk for sigils. The dead carried artifacts—both natural and constructed—as well as Fixed goods, man-made items that had been dragged far enough through the veils that they could be used by both the living and the dead.

While personal electronics were very popular, it was difficult to Fix them: They were mobile, not associated with a single place or person. Still, I saw several stalls that claimed to have Fixed versions of the latest phones, tablets, and mini-computers.

After the Pachinko machines and electronics came spice alley. I could almost remember what it smelled like: sweet fennel, exotic cumin, and the omnipresent sour smell of Chinese medicinal powders.

Just beyond the alley lay the general market. Vendors sat behind wooden tables scattered with rows of the latest faux-designer purses, pleather wallets, cutsie plush animals and ostentatious jewelry.

Toni waited for me at the far southern entrance, where a temple store displayed their goods—everything you needed to be a good Buddhist crammed into six square feet of space. The front display held dried herbs, while behind it were nestled packages of seasoned tofu: Faux-meat bearing such elegant names such as mountain-top goat meat, blue-sea swimming sunfish, and laughing pork shoulder. Long skinny altars, lotus blossom lamps, scratchy black cotton monk robes, and cheap Chinese slippers took up the rest of the space.

Toni looked as beautiful as always, wearing that dress that hugged her curves and heels that showed off her legs. It didn't matter to me that she could never change into anything else. If I had breath, the sight of her would have always taken it away.

In her life, Toni had been a thief, specializing in exotic gems and jewelry. Now, she focused on artifacts and art.

I didn't know what semi-legal or even illegal activities she was up to—I never looked too closely. I wasn't really a police officer any more, and even when I'd been alive I'd crossed more than a few legal lines myself.

"*Paisano*," Toni said warmly as I came up.

Ghosts could easily cause shivers in the living and the dead: None could raise the temperature in a room like Toni's happy smile could.

If I'd had a heart, she would have already stolen it.

"It's good to see you, Toni," I told her, coming close.

We did air kisses—something I would have laughed myself silly over if someone had suggested it when I'd been alive.

But ghosts could only touch things that had been Fixed. We certainly couldn't touch each other. It was one of the few ways Toni and I could show affection for each other.

"How goes your night?" Toni asked, a little too nonchalantly. She bent close to look at a Fixed status of a Buddha, sitting cross-legged, an artificial glow emanating from him: I wondered if the effect was just for us, and what the living saw.

"It's been fine," I told her, also trying to play it cool. "How about yours?"

Toni stood up and leaned closer, lowering her voice to a sibilant whisper. The living would be repelled by the slithering tones, while it only sent a slight chill up my spine. "Old Lee claimed he had a Fixed version of the latest iPhone."

"Really?" I asked, impressed. The phone itself was just a bracelet. The right combination of movements or spoken words made it project a button field that the living could use to dial a number or surf the internet. The dead, with our ectoplasmic flesh, couldn't interact with projected displays. They needed to be physical to be Fixed.

"He was exaggerating," Toni said with disgust.

I tsked. "He should have known better."

Many vendors liked doing business with ghosts, as the dead tended to have enough money for upmarket goods. But a business person lied or cheated a ghost at their own risk.

It was just our nature to be vengeful.

"He might know better now," Toni admitted, sounding satisfied.

"But that wasn't the only thing you've been up to tonight, is it, my dear?" I asked as we walked up the street, the furniture stalls giving way to racks of clothes, cheap knockoffs and expensive fakes, and row upon row of the latest graphic T, flared jean, or neon hoodie.

"I don't know what you're implying," Toni said, failing to keep a slight smile from the corners of her lips.

"Mrs. Lorenzo?"

"Aye," Toni said, her smile brightening. "She's energetic, no?"

"That's one word for it," I said dryly.

"Admit it. You liked her," Toni teased.

"I'd call it something different," I warned her.

"But you took her case, yes?" Toni asked eagerly.

"Why is it important to you?" I asked, stopping beside a rack of off-white strings that supposedly made up the most trendy turtlenecks. They looked like unfinished nets to me.

Toni shrugged. "I was just trying to help out a friend."

"Really." I didn't believe her. Not even a little.

However, I also respected her enough to leave her with her secrets.

"So where are these ferrymen?" I asked as we started walking again.

"Shhh," Toni said, looking around.

No one was paying any attention to us.

"You do know, don't you?" I asked after she still hadn't responded.

"No."

I blinked at her. "Really?" With her contacts, I always assumed Toni knew everything and everyone that affected the ghost community.

No," Toni repeated. "I do know someone, though. Who can help."

"But?" There had to be more.

"He won't deal with me," she said, pouting now.

"Why—never mind. I'll go talk with him."

Toni gave me her sunny smile, the one strong enough to almost warm a ghost's vacant heart. "I knew I could count on you, *paisano*."

There was yet another game being played, I knew.

But Toni knew me, her mark, too well.

I'd never let her down.

Toni led me into the heart of the night market, past the stalls of clothing and electronics, into the farmer's market portion. There had been a few ghosts gaping in the other sections, enviously peering at technology they could never touch or clothes they could never wear. Here, we were the only two, surrounded by wooden stalls heaped with bitter greens, cabbages, melons, berries and other food that was useless to us

"His name is Wix," Toni told me as we walked.

"Weeks?"

"Wix," she said, emphasizing the ending, drawing out the *sch* sound. "He's the liaison officer. You show respect."

"Don't I always?" I teased. Then I thought about what she'd just said. "Wait. An officer? Like, in the mafia?"

I knew that Toni was Italian: was this someone from her past? Had she been associated with the mafia when she'd been alive? Or was she doing jobs for them now, in her death?

Toni gave a disdainful sniff. "No. Triad. Asian." She looked at me. "This won't be a problem, I hope."

"No, no," I told her. I was in Vice back in the day, not organized crime. We'd had a few run-ins with gangs and the Triad, but I'd never worked either with or against them.

"Good," Toni pronounced. She turned down a narrow path between stalls. Bright Asian pop music blared from tiny speakers sitting on a table, surrounded by colorful radishes and carrots, leafy fennel, bright turnips, and gnarled ginger.

A middle aged Asian man with large gold aviator glasses sat behind the table. His hair was jet black and his teeth astonishingly white, with a pronounced gap between the first two on the top row. His face was flat and round, with a smattering of freckles across his cheeks and nose. He wore a plain white T-shirt and an oversized gold wristwatch.

"*Hau la*," he told Toni as she came up. "How goes it, love?"

His accent was impeccably British.

"Wix, always a delight," Toni said.

The smile she gave him wasn't anywhere near as warm as the smiles she gave me. It made me more wary.

"This is the friend I told you about," she continued. "Andy, Wix."

I nodded his direction. Though I couldn't shake his hand, I suspected his grip would be European, strong and firm, instead of Asian, gentle and two-fingered.

"Always a pleasure to meet a friend of Antonia's," Wix said. The smile he gave was just as fake as Toni's. "What can I do for such interesting companions?"

I didn't like the way he looked between Toni and I, seeking our secrets.

The dead have never really trusted the living.

However, there wasn't much I could do.

"You have a great standing in the community," Toni said, "And you are, yes, reasonable."

"No, no," Wix said, holding up his hands and shaking his head. "I am a simple shop keeper."

"But people still listen to you," Toni said. "And seek your council."

"It is nothing," Wix insisted. "I am honored that any would even remember me."

I rocked back on my heels, determined to be polite, no matter how many rounds of, "Oh, I'm not worthy" these two were about to play.

Toni, though, was clearly enjoying this. "But such a great man should have time to think, to ponder, the great things, the big ideas."

I was never going to understand her.

"It would be our honor to help such a man, to smooth out, little problems, in his way," Toni continued.

"To help out a fellow traveler, either in this life or beyond, is one of the true blessings," Wix said, bowing and nodding.

"Then let us help you," Toni said. "Let us remove this tiny impediment from your path."

"The wise man steps around such things. Still, I am curious. What would you help me with?" Wix asked.

"Ah, just a little thing. The two called the ferrymen."

I was surprised at how blunt she sounded after all the flowery praise.

I also hadn't signed up for dismantling a smuggling operation, just to free one soul.

"I have no argument with them," Wix said. "Why would you label them an impediment to my path?"

"A garden, it has only so many flowers," Toni said, warming to game again. "You are a great gardener. You only take the blossoms that are ripe, no? And nurture the plants. While they, they would rip the roses out by the roots."

"Eh, eh," Wix said, sucking air through the gap between his teeth and rocking back and forth. "The ferrymen are powerful," he said after a few more moments.

"And hidden," Toni said pointedly.

"I see," Wix said, looking between us again. "They interfere with your business, don't they?" he asked Toni.

"Business? What business? I run an art gallery," Toni said dismissively.

I knew Toni was lying, but her other activities had never been an issue.

Besides, it was hard enough to make a living as a ghost.

"And you?" Wix asked, looking at me.

I shrugged. "I'm curious about their location. It's for a case."

"Not for Antonia?" Wix asked, puzzled.

"No. I was the one who asked her if she could help." I

purposefully left out the relationship between Mrs. Lorenzo and Toni. That was no one's business but our own.

"I see, I see," Wix said. He brought his hands up, palms together, as if praying, touching his fingers to his lips, rocking and thinking again. "I will tell you their location," he told me after a moment. "But you can't tell Antonia."

"What?" Toni asked, indignant.

"How would you stop me?" I asked, curious.

"You are," Wix paused, looking me up and down. "A man who keeps his word. His promise. I need no binding or Seal. Just your word. And I will know if you break it."

Toni glared at me. "You cannot do this without me. We will find another way, *paisano*. Come."

I suspected she might have been right.

I also suspected that any other information we got would be tainted by Wix. He was a spider, his web flung far and wide.

"Tell me where the ferrymen are," I said quietly. "And I will give you my word that I won't tell Toni."

"Don't do this," Toni warned.

She didn't seem to be playing any con—she seemed serious.

Something else was going on between Toni, the ferrymen, Mrs. Lorenzo and Wix, some other long grift that I was stumbling across, a single track in a giant field of criss-crossing trails.

"I won't tell her," I said again.

"I believe you," Wix said solemnly, slowly standing. "Please, come back here," he added, moving aside a crate full of crinkling dried noodles. "You can meet up with your lady friend again later."

"Or not at all," Toni said. She gave me a curt nod, then gloriously strode off, her simmering rage giving her an extra glow.

She was magnificent.

"Come closer," Wix said.

Said the spider to the fly.

I didn't trust Wix, but I knew that his information would be solid, something I could work with.

Feeling like the narrow aisle was a Portal, and I was about to step Beyond, into Hell, I still followed him.

I knew I'd regret this case.

BEHIND THE NEXT STALL WAS A CLOSED OFF SPACE. WIX lifted the thick black curtain and showed me in. Though the pop music still played outside, the curtain dampened the sound.

Boxes with colorful labels in streaming Chinese characters were stacked floor to ceiling. A flat screen TV hung from one wooden wall, silently showing an Asian soap opera from long ago in a time of warriors, magic, and fantastically gaudy costumes. A small cot lay under the TV for quick naps and easy viewing.

"Excuse the informal setting," Wix assured me as he gestured for me to sit.

Normally, the living weren't comfortable being up close and personal with the dead. But Wix not only appeared unfazed, he sat down right beside me on the bed.

"Toni does exaggerate," Wix assured me. He reached up on the shelf beside us, bringing down a small wooden box with an intricately linked gold chain painted on the top.

"The ferrymen are not as much of an impediment as Antonia supposes," Wix explained, running his hands over the box in his lap. "They've been *allowed* to continue. But they have been...pushing their boundaries. Overstepping. Coming closer than they should. They need a lesson. Yes."

I knew that wasn't the full reason why Wix had offered to help me. I was only seeing the shadow play on the wall of the cave.

"Friends, they help each other, eh?" Wix asked, giving me a smile a used car salesman would have been proud of.

"What exactly are you asking me to do?" I growled deliberately.

Wix didn't seem to pale as much as the living usually do when faced with such ghostly subsonics. Maybe it was his darker skin, maybe it was the box in his hands.

Or maybe Wix was different, more different than I'd realized.

"Now, no need for that," Wix laughed. "I'm happy to help. Happy to help. Without a favor in return. But," Wix paused, studying his hands, seeming to consider his words. "I think returning the favor, and really, it's such a small thing, it's just the right thing to do. And you like to do the right thing, now, don't you?"

Wix looked up abruptly. His black irises were suddenly ringed with gold.

Wix was very different indeed. I wondered if his appearance had any effect on the living, persuading them to act against their better judgment.

Now, the dead didn't laugh. But I gave my closest approximation to a chuckle and repeated his words back to him, "Now, now, no need for that."

Interesting how my trying to impersonate the living disturbed Wix more than my natural ghostly skills.

"It has no effect on you," Wix said, leaning closer, peering carefully at me. "Perfect."

Wix shoved the box into my lap. On automatic reflex, I took it. The box was Fixed, but only barely. The wood felt slick and cold in my hands, a very interesting sensation, particularly since the dead could feel very little.

"What is this?" I asked, peering more closely at the painted design on the cover.

"A container," Wix said. "I need you to take it to the ocean, and open it, there."

"What's in it?" I asked.

Wix reached over and opened it. A golden haze flowed out,

immediately attracted to Wix, flowing into his hands and outlining them, like some sort of living glove. He rubbed his hands together, caressing them, trailing his fingers over the living gold covering.

"She needs to be free," he said tenderly. "But she won't leave me. She needs the ocean to draw her away."

Again, I had the strong feeling that Wix wasn't telling me the whole truth.

"She's an *ao*," Wix volunteered at my puzzled look. "Sorry, I'm not sure how to translate that into English. Sea creature, perhaps?"

He was lying. I was certain of it. She was much more than a mere denizen of the sea.

"In return for releasing her, I will give you the exact location of the ferrymen," Wix said as he reluctantly positioned his hands over the box and started brushing the gold off.

I stared intently at the pooling gold coil. I didn't get a feeling of evil flowing from her, like I had from Simon's artifacts from Beyond the wrong veil. No, I felt something very different.

This creature wasn't the same as Betsy, but they had a kinship.

"All right," I told Wix as he closed the box. "I'll do it."

While the box didn't grow heavier, it did grow noticeably colder again.

Wix looked at me sharply. "You will promise? Give me your word? Swear on your bones?"

There was very little the dead held precious, particularly the older dead: they'd seen everything come and go over many lifetimes.

We held our bones sacred. The best way to drive a ghost to revenge would be to do something to her bones.

"I swear. On my bones."

The silence grew between us, while the actors in the soap opera above us, wearing costumes bright enough for even a ghost to notice, flew through endless groves of bamboo.

"So, where are the ferrymen?" I asked eventually.

Wix gave me a predatory grin, showing all his flat teeth.

"On the water, of course."

BECAUSE MY DEATH RESEMBLED MY LIFE, IN THE AREA OF no decent luck, the ferrymen's boat wasn't on any convenient water, like Lake Washington or Lake Union. Hell, I would have been happy with one of the local canals. No, they were up in the Strait of Juan de Fuca, off the coast of Port Townsend.

As a ghost, I couldn't drive myself there. It was too long of a distance to cover on foot: despite being able to *flow* and move faster than the living, it was still too far away.

Which left public transportation, resulting with me standing on a pier in the gray morning fog. Though the bone numbing cold couldn't seep under my skin, like it could the living, it still looked damp and miserable enough to make me wish I could wear a jacket or even a scarf. The water stretched out brown and dirty under the mist, lapping at the pier with small slapping sounds. Some sort of moss or algae crept up the wooden sides, and I was glad I really couldn't smell it.

At least three dozen other ghosts waited with me. I had assumed there wouldn't be many others, given that there was a single ferry that took ghosts. Also, because most of my kind didn't travel. However, there appeared to be plenty of lost souls who were willing to be drawn away from their bones and suffer the constant longing for them.

The ferry, as it pushed its way out of the fog, glistened with the half light that came from an artifact being Fixed.

Why hadn't they just Fixed some seats? Why did they have to Fix the entire boat?

I brought Betsy up to get a better picture. She seemed warm in my hands. I knew it was just my imagination—just as I hadn't really been cold, she couldn't really make me feel heat.

It was still a comforting illusion.

Betsy's pictures were like a spectralgraph. They showed the supernatural influence on artifacts.

As I suspected, the ferry lit up like a Christmas tree. Not only was she Fixed, but spelled as well: Protection spells and ossifying charms and who knew what else.

It suddenly made me appreciate the ferrymen more, if this was what they had to do to their ship to transport ghosts on them.

The bellowing of the ship's horn raised the gate at the pier and the ghosts flooded onto the boat, through what had been the car ramp. Easier, I supposed, than Fixing the gangplank and bridge above us where the pedestrians usually came onboard.

The ship rocked as we boarded, as if struck by an unexpected swell. Was that a reaction due to being Fixed? Or something else?

We ghosts drifted up the stairs, past the closed and decommissioned snack bar, the tiny tables and ripped plastic benches, up to the sun deck, the irony of the name not lost.

I was surprised to see the boat was moving moments after we'd boarded. The purring engine had slid us out so smoothly I hadn't noticed the transition. I moved to the back of the boat, as had most of the others, looking toward my beautiful Seattle, sparkling in the fog and rain. The dim morning light hid any dirt or decay, and it appeared as perfect as an artist's sketch of the city, all clean lines, square windows, and complementary angles.

We slid past the marching rows of crate loaders, poised like graceful beasts, sliding their semi-truck-sized boxes from ship to shore.

It wasn't until we were about halfway across the Puget Sound that I felt the tugging on my soul: I was moving too far away from my bones. The water made the connection seem tinny and hollow.

I knew it would only get worse, the farther out I went.

While most of the others stayed at the back, I wrenched myself away and went to the front, to see where we were going.

One of the crewmembers stood directly in the center of the forward deck, against the railing. It couldn't have been comfortable for her: the wind whipped at her gray curls, pressing her neon orange-and-yellow-safety vest flat against her chest. Her hands looked red, chapped, and cold. But she still leaned forward, into the wind, a huge smile on her face.

I came up and stood beside her. I didn't know if she wanted company, or if one of my kind would even be considered company.

After a few long minutes of the wind punishing her and me wishing I could feel it, even a little, she turned and asked, "First time?"

"Yeah."

"Tourist? Or business?"

"Business. Ghosts travel as tourists?" I didn't think any ghost voluntarily traveled.

"You're headed to Port Townsend, then," she said, nodding.

"Yes," I told her slowly, surprised. "Do most ghosts do business in Port Townsend?"

"Fair few, yeah," she said. "I figure it's because it's said the ghosts outnumber the living up there."

I didn't know. I hadn't bothered looking up anything about my destination beyond how to get there.

"Old town," she added. "Lots of bones."

While that was possible, it didn't seem likely. Maybe the town itself was dying, the young people leaving, while the ghosts stayed.

"It's why we added the ferry leg, all the way up the coast to there."

"Why is there only one ghost ferry? It seems, well, popular."

"Takes a lot to hold a boat together under the weight of ghosts. Don't do it right, you'll tear a ship asunder."

"Really?" That didn't make sense.

"Puget Sound is a complex system of tides, currents, and winds. The water moves constantly, circling. And it's fresh water up top, from the rivers and rainfall. The salt water, which is more dense, lays further below."

I blinked and rocked back on my heels. "That's why you had to Fix the whole boat, then, isn't it? It's like fresh running water out there."

Not all the myths of what stopped the dead were true, but running water was an effective barrier: The more fresh, the more effective it was.

"The scientists declare it as salt water, but yeah, there's enough of a mix that your kind's sensitive to it. Summer time's better: it's more salt than fresh. But once the winter rains start, the mix changes. Spring's the worst, when the snow melts in the mountains and all the water floods into the Sound from the rivers."

That brought me to another thought. "What if this was true salt water? Like the ocean?"

"Wouldn't have to Fix and spell the whole boat."

"What about the Strait of Juan de Fuca?"

"More salt than fresh, particularly this time of year."

Was that why the ferrymen had parked their boat up there? Maybe they'd sailed up the coast from Mexico, staying in salt water, and only came in as close as they'd dared.

"Do you maintain the spells?" I asked, gesturing at the intricate netting and seashell sigil that hung from the rail, holding a spell that prevented a soul from spilling out over the water.

"Sure do," the woman said, her smile turning sad. "Would have been burned as a Witch in the old days, or persecuted as a lesbian fifty years ago. Now, I work as a civil servant, making my ship safe for ghosts."

I didn't know what to say. "At least it's progress?" I ventured.

"It's something," she said, turning away and heading back

inside the cabin, leaving me alone, pulled apart from my bones, only a long, lonely trip ahead of me.

THE GHOST FERRY STOPPED AT BREMERTON, BAINBRIDGE Island, Whidbey Island, then finally, Port Townsend. The boat rocked each time the ghosts flowed off and on, making me reconsider the weight of our collected souls.

Victorian houses in white, red, and gaudy pink stared down on the harbor from the top of nude cliffs. Wooden ships, going from two-men to ones that were truly ocean going vessels littered the cove, anchored all across it, as well as taking up every available berth. The ship yard stretched to the south of the pier, with boats raised up on lifts, upside down, showing their bones. I could easily imagine the smell of the caulk and freshly cut wood.

The boat bobbed as we ghosts left. I turned to wave to the crewmember I'd met, but she was already recasting one of the protection spells, her hands glowing with that strange half-light, her tight curls sparking.

She'd been right, though: most of the ghosts from the ferry got off at Port Townsend. Many of them were greeted by local ghosts. At first glance, the men merely seemed formally dressed. Only when I looked more closely did I realize they wore period pieces: cravats, linen shirts, and sweeping jackets.

I saw many soldiers too, with double-breasted jackets, brass buttons, long trousers, and black boots that held their shine even in death.

I was surprised so many had stayed from so long ago: I'd heard of a few here and there, but in this single small town, there were dozens.

Had the town been particularly evil? Or the wars so rotten?

Wix had told me where I'd find the ferrymen—in a bar

uptown, above the main drag, down in a basement, not well marked from the street. I had hours to kill before then.

I took some pictures of boats in the harbor, hoping that part of Wix' information had been out of date, and the ferrymen had moved their boat into the cove.

No such luck. There were some minor spells or artifacts on a few, but the boat I was looking for wasn't here: it was too close to the Sound, the water, too fresh.

If I was right, the ferrymen's boat needed more salt water, so straight north I went.

It wasn't too hard to find, or maybe like just attracts like. The boat was anchored out in the Strait, no pier around, or any other boats. I had no idea how I would get out there. It lit up in the picture I took of it, like bright search lights had been turned on it.

The boat was at least fifty feet long, and even from the shore I could see the spells along the rails that would stop any ghost from crossing. It had both engines and sails, able to handle anything. The deck was a deep yellow color, like it had been bathed in mustard, also a good deterrent for the dead. It sat oddly low in the water: I wondered if that was to keep the hull, and those things *Sealed* there, closer to the ocean waters.

I wandered from the shore through the park made out of the old fort that had been there, with battlements poured from concrete and steel bunkers for the great guns.

That was where I found the first cemetery. The soldiers kept to themselves there, and I would swear the smoke belching from their Portals still stank of coal and burning boats.

As I wandered, I found two more graveyards, where the ladies in their day dresses still promenaded. I didn't see their Hells, but they had to be worse than the bustles and tight corsets some of the women still wore.

I suspected these finely laid out graveyards were the real reason why there were so many ghosts here: like the town, when the Great Depression hit, the dead were left on their own, their bones, undisturbed.

Since I was here, I did go to one of the tourist spots, an old castle that had been turned into a hotel and restaurant. It was empty of ghosts, of course: for a while, it had been a Jesuit college, more deadly than any Hell to a ghost.

After night had fully taken hold, I made my way uptown. While some restaurants were still open, and the tourist strip downtown was still lively, the rest of the town had shut down.

Even with my muted vision I could see the deeply red color of the door of the bar. Instead of being warm, like Betsy, it pulsed, like lava.

I still pushed through it, though.

The bar looked perfectly ordinary. Blue, white, and red neon signs advertising different national liquors hung behind the bar, while the beer handles for the various brews on tap looked like a menagerie, with a dragon, a growling bear, and an unnaturally friendly dog. Dozens of bottles lined the lighted shelves.

Sitting on the bar itself was a gray bucket shining with that light of the Fixed—ghost rocks.

My appreciation for the town and this bar in particular rose considerably.

As a ghost, I couldn't drink or eat anything. Ghost rocks were a special type of Fixed whisky blocks that rattled when you shook them. It was a comforting sound, though the living sometimes complained that they sounded like rattling bones.

I sat down at the one Fixed stool at the bar and ordered myself a glass of ghost rocks, then turned to look at the rest of the bar.

Two large pool tables took up most of the space on the floor. In a semi-circle above them were stuck booths and tables, perfect for heckling the action below. Everything was made of blond wood, while almost all the lights were red. Nothing seemed particularly Hellish, though.

Maybe the owner just really liked red.

The ferrymen were actually easy to spot, slouching in a booth just off the center, close to the pool tables. Not because they were Mexican in a town of white folks, no, because they were *different*.

They looked like half-ghosts, like somehow their flesh had been Fixed.

I didn't know what they were. But Wix, or Mrs. Lorenzo, or, Hell, even Toni, would have said something if they weren't human, right?

I watched them interact with the world. They could pick up normal glasses, and more importantly, drink from them.

So they had to be living.

But they looked like the dead, had that same glow I did in the weird red lighting.

I tried to take a surreptitious picture of them with Betsy. But as soon as I brought her up, they both snapped their attention to me.

I gave them a hapless wave and took the picture anyway.

As they rose from their booth. I quickly glanced at the shot. They looked much more human when seen through Betsy's eye. What was telling was that they each wore amulets around their necks and wrists, and probably their ankles as well.

I was sure that was what was protecting them.

"Tourist, yes?" asked the shorter one as they drew closer. He wore his hair in a bowl cut, with bangs over his eyes and shaved midway up the back of his skull. He was in a faded cotton shirt with a flannel pattern on it, jeans, and boots.

"Yes," I said, nodding as I lowered Betsy down, cradling her in my hands, needing to protect her.

These two were as evil as Simon's artifacts, and as unnatural.

"Not many like you, tourist," said the other, his accent thick. He was taller, with skin ravaged by acne and shoulder length, greasy hair. His white T-shirt proclaimed, "TEH BRAINS" with an arrow pointing up.

"Also business," I said with a casual shrug.

"Business?" They both perked up.

"Artifacts," I lied.

"Yes, you, fancy camera," the short one said.

"Not for sale, our artifacts," the tall one said seriously. "But —you could make one!" He broke into a strange laugh, one that sent shivers down my spine: half ghost, half human.

His partner also laughed. He picked up the amulet around his neck, and I finally got a better look at it. It was shaped like a puzzle piece from a child's jigsaw puzzle, with gaudy green and red lines running across it, some sort of modern art.

It chilled me to my bones, waiting for me all the way back in Seattle.

The ferryman looked at his amulet, then at me. "Yeah. You fit, right in here," he told me, pointing to one of the looping holes, giving me a predatory smile.

Suddenly, Mrs. Lorenzo's stories of artifacts that were too strong, made from the souls of ghosts, made sense.

"Better here," I said, patting the solid wood of the Fixed bar. I picked up my ghost rocks and swirled them, clanking them together loudly.

It didn't seem to have the same calming effect on them, instead, they both took a step back.

"Keep your business to you," the tall one said, circling his finger in the air at me.

"I will," I assured them with a good ghostly growl.

As I expected, they didn't even appear to hear it.

"*Buenas noches*," I added with a nod.

"Eh, *buenas noches*," they said in unison, giving me the once over one more time before heading out.

I turned back to the bar and swirled the ghost rocks a little harder.

The damn ferrymen were untouchable. Their amulets would protect them from the dead, and quite possibly, from the living as well. They were half-ghost, without the fear of Portals or Hell.

They'd been able to attack ghosts, too, steal their souls from them.

Yet, somehow, in order to free Pepe, I was going to have to deal with them.

AFTER MY GHOST ROCKS HAD MELTED, I ORDERED ANOTHER. Not because I felt like sitting in a stuffy, crowded, overly loud bar, but because if those two ferrymen intended me mischief, I wanted to give them time to grow bored and leave before I came out.

I didn't know how they'd made their amulets. Maybe they needed the bones of the ghost. Or maybe they had banishment guns, effective for disassembling a ghost, and could then catch the soul as it left.

It was a strange feeling, to suddenly be cautious. I almost enjoyed it as I sat and watched the dance of humanity—the coy attraction dance between pairs, the sparked animation of drunken debate, the ancient couples who communicated entire conversations through a raised eyebrow or half a smile.

When I walked out of the fetid air and into the cool night, my attention was immediately snagged by cigarette butts across the street. They still had a lingering glow to them: the ferrymen had been waiting. I scanned the area carefully, first with my naked eye, then with Betsy's, but no one remained.

I still used caution on the way back out to the point, flowing as only a ghost can, moving with unhuman speed through the empty streets.

The ferrymen's boat glowed like a beacon across the dark waves, a siren's call for drowning sailors and lost souls. I still didn't see a way out to the boat, or even a way to combat the ferrymen themselves, bastardized ghosts that they were.

It all came down to their amulets. I couldn't remove them: Even if I could find a Fixed knife some place, I had little training in hand-to-hand combat. As a police officer, I was trained to disarm combatants, not cut off vital parts.

Plus, which was most important? The necklace? The bracelets? Could I remove just one and would the system fail? Or did I need to remove all three? Or even all five, if they did have anklets as well? Plus, once I removed their protection, haunting someone took some time. They'd have to be trapped or incapacitated somehow, while still conscious.

There were too many things I didn't know and I had no way of finding out.

As I turned to go, I heard a crackling noise, like fireworks in the distance. I stared in amazement at the ocean: I'd never heard it make such a noise before.

The next wave rolled forward. Men started marching out of the water. The ghost platoon wore the uniforms of more than one era, going from powdered wigs to desert camouflage.

How could they cross the water?

Then I realized they were emerging from the ocean.

Salt water, not fresh.

I looked beyond them to the ferrymen's boat, and a plan began to form.

I FOLLOWED THE SOLDIERS BACK TO THEIR CEMETERY, politely ignoring the massive cannons and burning ships that filled their Hells. The neat rows of white grave markers held their own glow in the dark night. Other ghosts from the town had gathered there as well. If the dead could have enjoyed such things, I would have called it a party.

Instead, it was merely a polite gathering of gentile folk.

As a police officer, I'd never been afraid of the limelight. It had brought me grief with more than one lieutenant.

But death changed a person. It took more will than I'd

expected to step into the center, clear my throat, and say, "Excuse me. May I have your attention?"

If I could have sweat, it would have been pouring down my sides. If my temperature could have changed, my hands would have been cold and clammy.

Being the focus of so many ghostly stares did, however, manage to send a shiver down my spine.

"I am Andrew Collin, former police officer with the Seattle police force," I said in my most formal manner.

Introductions were very important to older ghosts. Though Toni teased me about not knowing anything about the ghost community, I had paid attention to that.

"Now, I work as a private investigator, helping the living and the dead alike."

Though ghosts didn't have that many tells, I still knew I'd sparked their interest. No one was looking away and it felt as though the fires of Hell dancing in their Portals had died slightly.

"There's a boat off the coast—"

"The ferrymen," one of the soldiers interrupted, stepping forward. He wore the powdered wig of some ancient high rank. His uniform jacket was pristine with criss-crossing sashes and polished buttons. His pants buckled at the knee, with long hose and buttoned boots.

The attention of the gathered ghosts snapped to him. He stood up taller as a result, as if he welcomed it.

Twisted bastard.

"Yes," I said, turning to face him and his death head's grin. "They have one of our own, trapped in a Sealed room against his will."

Their reaction was immediate: ladies gasped while both soldiers and gentlemen stepped forward, standing at strict attention, awaiting orders.

A ghost army had suddenly formed in front of me.

It was more terrifying than any Hell.

General Silas quickly organized the volunteers, getting the fire starters into the first wave, and then everyone else into, well, the second wave.

Literally.

As the ghosts gathered in their groups, Silas pulled me to one side, marching me over to another ghost who he introduced as Private Burke, who looked both shy and earnest at the same time. He wore an outfit I would have placed in the first World War, with a starched jacket buttoned up to his neck and a thin hat perched on his head.

Silas looked pointedly at Betsy, then up at me. "You know the water will ruin her," he said gently.

"I can't just leave her behind," I said, looking first at him, then at the private.

"I know, son," Silas said.

I bristled at his words, trying to attribute it to just the age difference: at least a hundred and fifty years separated our deaths. Maybe more.

"Private Burke volunteered to look after your property," Silas continued.

"She's more than that," I growled automatically.

"We know, son, we know," Silas said gently. It was the most quiet I'd heard him all night. "This is why you can entrust her to the private."

Private Burke suddenly stood taller, straighter, and grew more still, as if he'd been transformed into wood.

For a ghost, it was eerie.

"Why should I believe you?" I asked, already fiddling with Betsy's strap.

"I swear to you, on my bones," Private Burke assured me. "I won't fail you."

I wondered what Hell awaited the young man, what made

him so earnest, the echoes of previous failures and broken promises dancing all around us.

"I will hunt you down," I growled at him as I removed Betsy's strap from around my neck. "If there's a single scratch. I will force you through the nearest Portal. I know how to *touch* you, and I will end you if she comes to harm."

Private Burke gulped, turning more pale.

An impressive feat for a ghost.

Silas, however, just looked thoughtful.

"He will take excellent care of her, or he'll also face me," Silas assured me.

Against my better judgment, I handed Betsy to him, my neck and chest colder and more empty, missing her familiar weight.

Had I always been such a trusting fool? Or had death changed me?

GOING INTO THE OCEAN FELT SIMILAR TO GOING *DOWN*, into the ground. Scientists who have studied the phenomenon have reported that ghosts take on different shapes underground. Some become snakelike; others, more of an amorphous blob.

Me, I've always felt as though I grew round, with a hard skin, like a ping-pong ball. I didn't lose myself or any consciousness, but I was aware that I was very different underground than above it.

This, though, felt like going underground while on the drug Slide. Instead of a solid ball, I felt like tendrils of me trailed behind me, waving and fragile, like the leaves of a sea fern bathed in the tide.

I'd never tried crossing a running stream. I'd heard accounts of souls who'd lost their way, spinning strong enough to create deadly whirlpools, never able to find their way home. Even the call of their bones wasn't enough to draw them out.

The saltwater lessened the pull of my bones, back in Seattle. Instead of a rope, it thinned to mere wire. Everything else dimmed further, and a hopelessness pressed against me, as deadly as atmospheres of pressure to the living.

I may have turned back at that point, except for Silas. He knew how to lead souls. His own certainty gave him a glow that was easy to follow.

Slick fish passed by us in the depths. Litter from modern eras as well as ancient tripped us as we marched across the silty sands.

We did seem to gain weight in the water. I couldn't feel myself press against the ocean floor, but tiny puffs of soot released into the murky depths after we passed.

It gave me hope that this plan could work.

The first wave had gone before us, led by a vet from a modern era who'd seemed more cocky than most. Their job was to start a fire, and hopefully only one, that would separate the boat from its anchor.

Ghosts were the second most likely source of any fire now, due to our affinity to flames. I didn't believe the theories of Hellfire or that nonsense, though watching a ghost descend from the surface, with flame still blooming in his chest, giving his face a skeletal glare, did make me pause.

They didn't burn any of the rest of the ship, and seemed to have accomplished their mission without alerting the crew.

Silas directed the scouts next, judging the distance of the second group of ghosts to the nearest bank. Based on their reports, Silas arranged the rest of us in a loose triangle formation, just behind where the boat floated.

On command, we all *pushed* forward, as hard as we could, with hands and will, trying to influence the water around us, using the weight of our souls.

It wasn't much of a wave. Hardly noticeable from the surface.

But the boat, sitting low and now floating free, unmoored, started to move.

We reformed and pushed again, sending the boat around the tip of Port Townsend, leaving the Strait of Juan de Fuca and heading into the Pugent Sound.

Since we were so far below the surface, we couldn't sense the change immediately.

The ferrymen did, though. Screams echoed above us.

Silas and I exchanged a death's head grin before we *pushed* again, moving the boat further into the freshwater.

The amulets that protected the ferrymen from my kind made them too much like us: they couldn't cross over into fresh running water.

Splashes, followed by sinking figures, told us their fates, the amulets confusing them and forcing them overboard, into the depths to save them.

But they were too human to survive down here, too scared with an army of ghosts marching toward them to escape to shore.

Or maybe the poor souls who'd been forced to protect them were able to exert more control and held them still while we bore down on them, trampling *through* them and burying them in the silt.

———

LIKE THE OTHERS, I WALKED CAREFULLY OUT OF THE waves, ensuring that I had all my parts, that I hadn't left something vital trailing beyond, something to cause me to return again and again to the sea.

One of the dandies who'd stayed behind had already informed the coast guard of the abandoned ship. I was certain they'd find the Sealed room and free Pepe. Between Mrs. Lorenzo and Toni, I knew he'd stay in the country.

I was surprised at how dry I felt on the beach. I'd assumed

the sense of the water would have stayed with me, somehow. But it hadn't, and the call of my bones wrapped around me as tightly as any nose.

The beach was empty in the pre-morning light, the stones glistening with dew. The wind had died and the tide was quiet. We ghosts drifted through the park, past the officer quarters and training yard, the modern cars and old buildings, into the graveyard. The white markers glowed even brighter in the faint light, luminescent signs of past and present glory and failure.

I knew Hells Bells were approaching—every ghost could feel the start of the dawn. I wanted to get Betsy and find a dark corner where I could snooze for a while before catching the ferry home. Though ghosts had no bodies, we still needed rest, our brains and our wills required downtime.

Private Burke snapped to attention as we approached.

My rage boiled freely when I saw he was empty handed.

I pushed past Silas and bellowed directly into the face of the private. "Where is she?"

"It's not my fault," the private whispered. "She—"

"*You* were responsible," I said, pressing against him. My chest started to merge with his, a distinctly unsettling feeling.

I didn't care.

"I know, sir," Private Burke said.

If he could have sweat I'm sure I would have seen it streaming across his brow.

The private made a valiant effort to continue. "But she—"

"She?" I growled.

I was ready to take the private apart.

"*Paisano*. Really?" came a voice from behind me.

I whipped around. Toni came out from the trees, Betsy cradled in her hands.

I'm not ashamed to say I sagged in relief.

"Whoa, son," Silas said, reaching out to me but not touching me. "I'm glad the private didn't do something too foolhardy. Though your anger was a delight to see. A delight, I say."

I glanced at Silas, then shook myself and straightened up.

He was right. Ghosts rarely felt intently about anything.

But Betsy had changed me.

As had Toni.

I shivered with fear—was I growing more like Mrs. Lorenzo? I pushed the horrifying thought aside.

"Thank you, General Silas," I said, giving the old ghost an officer's salute, the highest compliment I knew how to give.

"Thank you, soldier," Silas said, saluting back. "I hope to see you again some day."

"Thank you, private," I added before I walked over to my best girls.

"Hi," I told Toni, almost shyly, as I held out my hands for Betsy.

"You softy," she said, handing me my camera.

We stood for a moment, each holding Betsy, our fingers almost touching, as close as we'd ever get.

If I'd had a heart, it would have found a new rhythm, one to match hers.

The moment passed. The tenderness washed off Toni's face as it had never been there.

"How did you find me?" I asked as I put Betsy's strap back around my neck.

"I have my ways," Toni said mysteriously.

"You had me followed," I guessed.

Toni angrily slapped my arm, her hand passing *through* me.

"What? Did I deserve that?" I asked, shaking my arm as my muscles reassembled.

"Yes," Toni said angrily. "I would never entrust your business to someone else. *I* followed you."

Maybe it was love.

143

"DO YOU WANT TO MEET PEPE?" TONI ASKED AS SHE walked back toward the trees where she'd been waiting.

I eyed the lightening sky. "Do I dare?" I asked. I was exhausted and not sure I could face any more adventures.

"Yes," Toni said with an exasperated sigh. "Mrs. Lorenzo is very important in our community. You should accept her thanks."

I didn't like the sound of that at all. But I agreed. I knew I'd follow Toni into Hell and back.

The bag Toni fetched was a fashionable shoulder bag, obviously Fixed, and probably hideously expensive.

It seemed overly full, not just of the mysterious items that made up a woman's purse, but with a box.

Toni saw me looking at it as we flowed out of the park and onto the residential streets. The old houses around us were just waking up, with one or two lights on, showing activity. A neighbor was walking their dog, and a couple of startled joggers crossed the street at our approach.

"Well?" she asked as we reached the main drag downtown. "Aren't you going to ask?"

As soon as she said that, I didn't have to. I knew what she carried.

I'd left it in my room at Mrs. H—'s establishment. Of course, I didn't have any locks on my door. Only a fool would try to disturb a sleeping ghost, or a ghost's things.

We were vengeful.

"Why did you bring it?" I asked, knowing she carried the box Wix had given me.

"We are at the coast, no? Easier with just one trip."

If I could have laughed, truly chuckled, I would have. "You couldn't open it."

Toni glared at me. "Why did Wix Fix the box so that only you could open it?"

"I have no idea," I said blandly, not telling her that I'd asked him to.

It was the only way to keep the contents inside of it safe.

Love, or the ghost equivalent, may have changed me, but it hadn't made me completely stupid.

Far out on the water, a rolling mist had gathered, blocking the view, making it seem as though we were at the end of the world. Close in, the water was smooth and clear, reflecting the tinted orange and pink sky of the coming dawn.

A collection of coast guard officers stood on the end of the pier, talking earnestly with one another. Just beyond them stood a pair of ghosts, who pushed their way *through* the men when they saw us.

While I didn't like the experience of passing through either the living or the dead, and it usually gave me pause, these two didn't slow down at all, or seem to notice the glares from the men.

I took a step forward, in front of Toni, as they bore down on us.

The one on the left was *huge*.

I wasn't a small guy when I'd been alive, and dead, I figured I was still at least six feet.

This ghost towered over me. And his companion, while she was shorter, had considerable girth.

Toni leaned forward and whispered in my ear, "Relax, *mio galante*. It's just the Lorenzos."

Since Mrs. Lorenzo had such a large personality, I'd assumed her Pepe would be tiny.

Instead, he was the biggest ghost I'd ever seen, a bear of a man. He wore a Mexican style, short-sleeved shirt, casual pants, and flip flops.

"Oh!" Mrs. Lorenzo exclaimed. "Thank you, thank you, thank you!" She reached forward, maybe to grab me and kiss me on both cheeks, but restrained herself at the last minute, clasping her hands in front of her chest and bowing her head at me.

"I, too, offer my thanks," Mr. Lorenzo said, his voice every bit as deep and gravely as his size would indicate.

"And now that the ferrymen are gone, we can resume our business!" Mrs. Lorenzo said with glee.

"If you ever need something, anything, carried or shipped, just let us know. Free of charge," Mr. Lorenzo said, nodding first at me, then at Toni.

Mrs. Lorenzo lost some of her glee at that, particularly after glancing at Toni, but hurriedly added, "Of course, Pepe, of course. You are right." Then she turned her calculating eye at me. "Unless you would like a job? Something more steady? You might have to travel, but," then she shrugged and indicated the pier, as if to say, here you are already.

Suddenly, it all made sense.

Mr. and Mrs. Lorenzo were planning on taking over the ferrymen's business, smuggling souls and who knew what else.

And Toni, well, my Toni was probably going to be using their services.

"No, no," I told them. "I like what I do. And I do need to get back to my bones."

Mr. and Mrs. Lorenzo both glanced involuntarily over their shoulders at the large box at the end of the pier.

Not a coffin, no, a handy travel box for Pepe's bones.

What had really been the precipitating event? Had Pepe's bones been on his own ship, and had he been hijacked by the ferrymen?

I didn't know, and I didn't want to find out.

Before we said our goodbyes, Toni insisted on a picture of her with the Lorenzos, then me, as if we were actually friends, meeting each other on vacation.

Then we headed back to the coast, our last task still at hand.

WE OPENED THE BOX ON THE WEST SIDE OF PORT

Townsend, however, the curl of gold in the corner couldn't be coaxed out.

Which meant yet more public transportation: this time, a sixteen plus hour series of bus rides, south to Tacoma, then west to Ocean Shores. We had no problem finding Fixed seats, and snoozed most of the way.

I learned I didn't miss my bones as much this trip. Maybe it was becoming habit through all this travel, maybe it was the amount of water, not land, between me and Seattle. Or maybe Toni made the difference.

The wind on the coast was relentless. Irritating sand blew *through* me. At least six inches of foam churned on the tops of the waves. When the water deposited a load, the wind picked up pieces of if, tumbling chunks of brown foam across the sand.

It wasn't my personal idea of Hell, however, I'm sure it was someone's.

Toni stood out on the beach, looking elegant, her high heels not sinking into the sand. A few of the women we passed, all bundled up, looked envious.

At the edge of the water, box in hand, Toni stopped me and insisted on taking another "vacation" shot.

When I opened the box this time, the gold strip streamed out, growing, becoming a long winding golden banner, shivering in the wind.

Then it expanded more, taking on features beyond a mere strip: snout, eyes, claws.

I dropped the box and took a step back as an ancient golden dragon took to the air, now swimming against the wind, heading straight west, going back to its home, somewhere in Asia.

"The Hell?" I asked Toni, barely drawing a breath as it undulated away.

Based on Toni's expression, if tears could have dripped down a ghost's face, they would have been.

"Wix is a liaison officer," she said eventually.

I gave a long, low whistle, and belatedly tried to take a picture.

I'd seen many things in my life, and even more strange things since my death, but nothing like this.

For the first time since I'd died, I had a sense of wonder.

The box was gone when I looked back at my feet, dissolved by the foam and wind, perhaps.

Toni and I were both silent for a long time, long after the gold strip had disappeared into the pale blue sky.

On the first long bus ride back, while Toni slept, I decided to look through the pictures on Betsy.

The first few were normal, well, normal enough photos of ships, the town, the ferrymen, Mr. and Mrs. Lorenzo with Toni, me with them.

The picture of me at the ocean side with the box in my hand wasn't normal.

Stretched out behind me, reaching toward the waves, floated a pair of broken, burnt wings.

I went back to the shot of me with the Lorenzos. Nothing unusual there. Or Toni standing with them, the box in her bag.

Still nothing.

Was this how Betsy truly saw me, and that the magic from the dragon had let her capture? The real me? A broken and bent creature, rejected by Heaven, reserved for Hell?

Were those really my wings? Had I taken a fall, and could I rebuild them, feather by feather, here on Earth? Or was this my state, now and forever, graceless and without hope?

I truly didn't know. But like all postcards from Hell, the photo was horrifying, while at the same time, too mesmerizing to look away from.

I looked at the last picture, which merely showed a golden strip flying above a gray ocean.

Maybe I'd imagined it all. But no, not that sense of wonder.

That possibility of hope.

I erased the photo of me so Toni couldn't see it.

But I did email it to myself first, calling myself all kinds of fool for doing so.

I couldn't kill that possibility, that slim chance of redemption that I really didn't believe in.

I couldn't stop myself from thinking that one day, I'd see those wings again, healed and new.

OF HEAVEN AND HELL

I WOULD HAVE KILLED FOR A GOOD FACIAL.

Not that I needed it. No, *amica*. As a ghost, my face never changed, not since I died.

I missed the pampering, though. The oils scented with mint and orange, the lime masks and the exacting *senorita* who, like an artist—a sculptor—made such perfection of my eyebrows.

I couldn't change my clothes or my jewelry. It was always the same white dress, the same diamond earrings, the same heels that no longer pinched my toes or hurt my back. Surprisingly, that didn't bother me, no, not as much as never getting another of Tess' special mani-pedis, with real milk, avocado, and almond butter. It was like walking through a vegetable buffet, but she performed miracles with my skin.

It was always the simple things, no?

Luckily, I looked good in what I could wear, and that was what was most important. A girl wants to turn heads, living or dead.

The night Rachel came to see me, I was not the only one people watched. My art gallery, *The Haunting Hour*, was hosting a performance piece directed by a local artist, a companion to the art on the walls.

I could lie and say it had great meaning, those actors all in white, like ghosts, rolling around on the warm wooden floor, entangled in a net made from red strings.

Truthfully, I think the living who pay for such things were a little crazy—looking for something outside to lift them, instead of finding such things in the traditional places, with family, friends, and the church.

Yes, I have always believed, though most would laugh to hear. I've never talked of it, and I didn't take communion anymore. But God still moved through my life.

I believe God was why Rachel came to me.

I hadn't realized she was a ghost. I would have thought that when she died, she would have passed directly Beyond, straight to Heaven. She hadn't lived such a life as I, acquiring baubles and pretties for clients, and rarely legally.

Or maybe Rachel had known more than any of us had realized of Yakob's—her husband's—business, the extra books and hidden accounts he kept for some of us.

I saw her the minute she stepped through the door.

Whatever she'd been expecting, it probably hadn't been a room full of both the living and the dead, watching men writhing on the floor.

I was proud I didn't laugh, because Rachel stood there, her mouth gapping, her eyes wide and unblinking, like a cartoon. Finally, she came back to herself, and merely looked bewildered and lost.

She'd been buried in a white, three-quarter sleeve sweater, over a stiff black dress that went up to her neck and down past her knees. Just looking at her made me uncomfortable.

Fortunately, she saw me as well, and made her way through the crowd. She kept looking at the dull human art and the squiggles and lines that were the best the dead could come up with. Blue-and-white harlequin sequined servers carried trays full of sparkling wine (for the living) and Fixed glasses with specially frozen ice for the rest of us.

"Rachel." I greeted her warmly, standing to kiss her cheeks.

Of course, I couldn't actually touch her. As a ghost, I could only touch those things that had been Fixed. But we air kissed, three times, as was the European custom.

"Antonia," she said, her eyes larger than I remembered, and so much darker than most ghosts. "You must help me."

I was surprised at how abrupt she was. With no hesitation, I asked, "What do you need?"

For some friends, there was no question. For Yakob—Rachel's husband—in his memory, I would help with anything.

"Yakob's picture. They've stolen it. I must get it back."

"Which picture? Who took it?" I asked.

Yakob had never collected fine art. He spent his earnings on vacations with Rachel and fine wine for their table.

"It's an old painting. Handed down to Yakob by his father, and his father before him."

I hadn't known Yakob had such an heirloom, but I knew that Yakob, like me, prized family above all else.

"Who took it Rachel?" I asked as the actors reached the high point of their piece, trapped, thrashing on the floor in a frenzy.

"The Nazis." Rachel said it with utter conviction, as if she would wager her soul that it was true.

I stared at her, finally seeing what was before me.

Rachel's eyes weren't just larger and darker than most: They also spun with a specific madness.

The Portal to Beyond had shown Rachel Heaven when she'd died, but she'd chosen to stay here instead, in this very specific Hell.

———

OF COURSE, I WENT TO SEE MY ANDREW AS SOON AS I could. He thought I teased him, sometimes, when I called him *paisano*, like *brother*, closer than *friend*.

And maybe I did, at the start. But he was the only one who truly deserved the title now.

He listened too much to what others told him, though he was never that straight and narrow, even when he'd been *polizia*.

If we'd been alive, he would have been my lover, my *confidante*. I would have shared everything with him: my body, my time, my life.

Since we were ghosts, all I could show him was my soul.

Fortunately, he was smart enough to realize that was enough, a gift he gladly shared in return.

We met late that night—the dawn hadn't come with her racket—but soon that howling would start, urging the dead to retreat.

He picked me up at the gallery and we walked, past the closed light rail station that even I, as a ghost, could see the bright red of, and into the park behind it, with the fountain and the old reservoir underneath.

We kept to the rock path, though the wet spring grass wouldn't have impeded me, despite my impractical heels. A flock of the little birds—chickadees and thrushes—made a racket from the still bare trees.

Of course, the homeless camping there didn't bother us. Our ghostly brethren needed to haunt something sometimes, and few stood up for those who didn't pay regular taxes.

Besides, we rarely scared them to death.

By the time we reached the far end, past the soccer field, and were turning back, Andrew was watching me with a concerned look on his face.

I realized I hadn't been speaking. Normally I had enough conversation for both of us.

Finally, I started. "An old...friend, I guess, came to the gallery tonight."

"Ah," Andrew said, nodding.

I was grateful for the space to continue. I did wonder,

sometimes, what my Andrew had been like, alive. Had he always been this patient?

I doubted it. He had more than one ex-wife.

Death did change a person.

"She wants my help. Someone—" I paused, and sighed. "Someone stole a painting from her. From her family."

"Why doesn't she go to the police?" he predictably asked.

"Why is it always the police with you? Can't a friend ask a friend for help?"

He merely raised an eyebrow and wisely didn't speak.

Just as I knew him, he knew me. I was delaying.

"All right," I grumbled. "She claims the Nazis stole it."

"Is she Jewish?" he asked as we walked silently along the path, only my memory supplying the sound of solid footsteps crunching on the loose rocks.

"Yes. And it was her husband's picture, from Yakob's family."

"When did the Nazis take it?"

I stopped, surprised. "You believe her?"

He shrugged. "There are some very old ghosts."

"She claims they stole it just before her death. It's why she refuses to go Beyond."

"Has she been looking for it for a long time?"

"Yes," I told him without hesitation.

There were times I didn't tell my Andrew the truth. It would have been cruel not to tell him of this—not given his insane niece.

"Why you?"

"I was her friend!"

Andrew shook his head. "She didn't come to you first. You were further down on her list."

I paused in the pre-dawn light, forcing myself to be still, though soon, Heaven itself would be screaming for me to go.

"Thank you, *paisano*," I told him sincerely.

I had only ever been a minor client of Yakob's. I hadn't met

Rachel many times—a few times at his office, out to dinner a few more.

I was going to have to see what his other, more important clients were up to.

And what had happened after Rachel had visited them.

I PROMISED ANDREW I WOULD BE CAREFUL. MORE than once.

It was touching, really. He was much more gentle in his death than I'd ever been in my life.

And now, in death, a woman had a right to protect herself, no? Her duty, even.

No matter what my Andrew thought (and so carefully never asked about,) I'd turned my back on the life I'd once lived. Sure, I sometimes took an odd job here or there, mostly to keep my hand in. But I never looked up any of my old clients. If I knew them after death, it was because they had looked me up, had gotten in contact with me.

Yakob had been discrete, had never advertised: a true gentleman, all word of mouth. The only reason I knew some of his other clients was because I had recommended them.

When Buster Miller had been alive, he'd run an upscale, legitimate bar in upper Queen Anne.

However, the poker games in the back weren't so legal.

Fortunately, for Buster, Andrew's boss, the head of vice in Seattle, was willing to turn a blind eye as long as he had a guaranteed seat at the Friday night game.

I'd never seen Andrew there. I doubted he knew about it. His vices while he'd been living had seemed to run to pretty girls and cigarettes.

Still, I insisted on going alone. Andrew was a proud man. Running into his old boss would have made him feel foolish.

It was why I had directed him to Simon's poker game,

though no one in the community had realized that Simon was not who he said he was.

Even today, people asked me of him. Even today, those of us who knew, watched more closely than even my Andrew was aware of.

God did not put us here to hurt this Earth or her people.

Besides, the uptown game would have been difficult for him to get to. The silly man had his pride, so he took busses.

Many cab drivers were superstitious. Andrew believed they wouldn't carry a ghost.

They would, or at least the black cabs had seats that were Fixed.

What he didn't know was how to pay them.

There was an abandoned track in one of the eastern suburbs, built by post baby boomers who never had their own boom.

These cabbies believed that to run into a ghost, or drive their cabs *through* them, used up all their bad luck. Some thought they were only allotted so many accidents per year by their demons or saints, depending on the cabbie.

So ghosts volunteered to take away their bad luck, their accidents.

The cabbies could use them all up on us, and never have one involving the living.

Some swore by it, saying they had fewer and fewer accidents as time went on.

I never believed it. It didn't feel like God's work.

But more than God moved through the world these days as well.

I only went the once: Then I found a suicidal young man, who was thrilled for the chance to pay for his sins.

Facing a racing car, with a madman behind the wheel, knowing they were about to drive through you, was as bad as it sounded. Even though I knew I would survive, it was frightening, and uncomfortable, your insides squished that way.

I didn't like it. I enjoyed the convenience, though, of a cab on call. I would only go back and do it again if I couldn't avoid it.

One of the black cabs waited for me at sunset. He introduced himself as Manny. He had the maniacal eyes of a fanatic below bushy black eyebrows. I was surprised by his turban: Most Sikhs didn't believe in killing, let alone driving a car through a ghost. His face was shorn clean, though, so maybe he was some other sect.

He set off at breakneck speed. If I hadn't already been dead, I would have worried. Instead, I held on and enjoyed the ride, first down from Capitol Hill, weaving around busses and cars, turning onto side streets every time the traffic slowed, then up and up Queen Anne Hill.

After the abrupt stop in front of Buster's new restaurant, Manny turned to look at me.

He paled but bravely handed me the ledger.

I stopped smiling, reminded again of how cruel it was that my glee frightened the living.

I put and X next to my name. I had few, very few, rides left.

In fact, much of book was now empty.

I was going to have to go talk with my young friend. Maybe he'd gotten bored and found something more exciting.

Or maybe he'd been a ghost for long enough he'd reached the stage of *ennui* that affected so many.

Manny uttered a blessing on me as I got out, in his native tongue.

I thanked him warmly for it.

God still moved through my life.

Buster's new restaurant and bar was actually a converted garage from the 50s. The floor was scuffed concrete and the shelves holding the liquor bottles were scarred, old, black metal. Even the bar itself was made out of fused car parts.

A line still went out the door. Supposedly, Buster made the best burgers in town. I would never taste one, but the rich scent of grilled meat that floated through the air was enticing.

I walked past the restaurant, down around the corner. Spring hadn't taken hold yet: The trees barely budded, and the living still bundled up in warm coats and scarves.

Of course I wouldn't have anyone drop me off exactly where I was going. I stopped at the entrance of the alley.

At least it was clean.

Alleys and back ways have always fascinated me—seeing the real lives of people, not the show they put on out front. To see the weeds that choked the back fence while the front lawn was still so trimmed, the strange Buddhist garden with status and floating lotus flowers, and the garage turned into a den with dark wood paneling, bookshelves, and heavy, leather, wingback chairs, more fancy than any room in the adjoining house.

The back of Buster's garage had two entrances. One was a solid metal door, the blue paint faded with sunlight and time, that bore a large sign proclaiming, "Employees Only."

Next to it stood a door that few saw.

I always meant to ask Buster to recommend his spell worker. The charm was so elegant, a simple, "Look Away" spell that tickled the edge of my thought, but not strong enough to give any of the dead pause.

The door was unlocked, of course. Who would bother a gathering of ghosts?

The smell of burgers was stronger here, layered with garlic and warm bread. It was almost enough to make a ghost hungry. Only the back had been divided into two levels.

A narrow wooden staircase led up to the loft. In the front, there was only a single story, the ceilings high enough to fit the cars on lifts.

It was a good, hidden place.

Something bothered me as I walked up the stairs. A difference nibbled at me, stronger than the bespelled door.

When I stepped onto the loft I finally realized what it was: All the railings had been removed. The loft opened up onto open space now. One wrong step and it was a long trip down.

That wouldn't be a problem for the dead. Had Buster had some disagreement with the living?

The center of the loft held a large round table, covered in green poker felt. Over a dozen ghosts sat there, holding cards and swirling glasses filled with ghost rocks—like scotch rocks— that could be chilled over and over again, that had the perfect sound (for a ghost) when shaken or swirled in a glass.

I didn't think that they sounded like rattling bones or chains. Ridiculous, that sort of stereotype of ghosts. To me, they sounded higher, like the joyful breaking of wine glasses at a feast.

Buster rose when he saw me, folding his cards and stepping out of the game.

"Antonia!" he said, coming forward.

He'd been such a handsome man, and he hadn't lost any of that as a ghost. I was sure he'd been teased for being a carrot top as a child, but as an adult, the color had mellowed and now glinted with a burnished gold. Death had paled his blue eyes, but his ghostly skin still held onto its freckles. He wore an open collar shirt with an old fashioned vest: I'd often wondered who'd dressed him for his death, or if he'd somehow managed to shuck the suit coat most men were buried in.

"My dear Buster," I said, giving him casual air kisses.

"What brings you to grace my humble garage with your beauty?" he asked.

If I hadn't known him to be such a snake, I would have been charmed.

"An old friend came to see me," I told him. "I thought, maybe she came to see you first."

"Francoise Beaker?" he guessed.

I raised an eyebrow at him. I hadn't even realized she was still with us.

Maybe I could recruit her against her uncle Simon…

I shook my head. I could deal with that later.

"No. Rachel Goldman."

I'd never seen a ghost grow pale before.

Yet, Buster replied, "Really? I haven't seen her."

"Please, Buster, we've been friends for too long."

"We were never friends, Antonia," Buster corrected gently. "Business rivals, perhaps."

"I'm hurt," I told him.

We hadn't been friends, true, but rivals? When had I ever bested him in business?

"The Briar piece," he added.

"A trifle," I told him, dismissing his claim like the nonsense it was.

He crossed his arms and glared at me.

I waited. I could be patient, no matter what my Andrew said.

Still, I was the one who broke. "You aren't going to let that stand between us now? Truly?"

Buster looked down for a moment, then up, his pale eyes sad. "Mrs. Goldman—what she's lost—if she ever had it—doesn't matter. What has it now…beware."

Buster abruptly turned and walked back to the poker game.

I felt adrift as the newly dead.

Nothing scared tough men like Buster.

However, not only was he scared, he'd been warned not to say anything.

Whatever, whoever, had Yakob's painting would find me more stubborn than scared.

OF COURSE, I WAS NOT ABOUT TO TELL MY ANDREW OF what I'd found.

Silly man would try to protect me.

However, God had other ideas.

My Andrew came by my gallery later that night. I was surprisingly busy: I had sold two paintings the week before, and the patrons had only arranged to pick up their pieces that night.

I wondered about the men they chose, with physiques more suited to body guard than cheap labor.

Were the art buyers afraid for their lives in this bustling part of Capitol Hill? Or did they foolishly fear the ghosts here?

No matter.

They paid well for mere scribbles, the only "art" the dead could produce.

I didn't like the way the two men looked around the shop. I recognized what they did. I had done that sort of looking myself when I'd been alive, in another line of work.

They wouldn't find any alarms, though, or cameras. There was a single spell, that I doubted they would recognize—a memory spell.

It captured more than just the face of all who came in: It trapped their "presence" as well, or, as the witch had described it, their spiritual signature.

If these two came back unannounced, they could take whatever they wanted.

Then I would hunt them down. The spell guaranteed I would find them.

Then they'd learn that ghosts could be very vengeful, indeed.

But that was a problem for another day.

Right then, I had Andrew looking worried, never a good thing.

As soon as the goons left, I turned to Andrew and said, "*Paisano*. We did not have a date that I missed, no?"

"No." He then gallantly offered, "But I would be happy to take you out later."

"Maybe later," I told him. "Now, tell me your news."

He hesitated.

"Come, *paisano*. *Mio gallante*. Your worry is all over your face."

"It's the Nazis," he blurted, then winced, as only one can when one speaks out loud what should be ridiculous.

"So they are real?"

"Yes and no. Are they really German Nazis, or even homegrown American skinheads or neo-Nazis? No." He shook his head. "They appear to be worse."

I cocked an eyebrow at him. The fascists had been bad, very bad, in my country. I had heard so many frightening stories about them while growing up.

What could be worse than men who wanted absolute rule through terror and torture of their fellow countrymen?

And the living thought ghosts were bad.

"They're still alive," Andrew continued. "But bespelled." He raised his serious eyes to mine. "They claim to be like vampires. That feed on ghosts."

I scoffed, but he didn't smile.

"You're serious."

He nodded. "They say they have charms—or something— that protects them from us, as well as spells that suck the energy out of the dead."

I would have scoffed again, but he had seen as many strange things as I.

Possibly more.

"What about the painting?"

He nodded again. "It's possible they took it. They say that's part of their power, these Jewish artifacts, 'their sweet anguish' powering them further."

"Did you talk with one of these…creatures?" I refused to name them, as that gave them power and history, when they were merely abominations.

"Nope." Finally, he smiled. "Found their web site. Or at least, a site that was about them." He grew serious again. "Has your friend always been in Seattle? Or has she moved her bones, traveled to other cities, to track them?"

"I don't know." It had never occurred to me to ask, but that would help explain why I hadn't known Rachel was a ghost, still with us.

"They've only recently come to Seattle, as far as I can tell. So did they follow her? Or did she follow them?"

"What do you mean?"

My Andrew was always so see-through when he tried to hide something.

"There isn't a dip in the ghost population after these 'vampires' arrive in a city. They don't seem to be feeding on ghosts until they disperse or somehow move Beyond."

Their sweet anguish. "So they steal from their victims, then stay close, to, to—"

"Drink their sorrow?" Andrew shrugged. "It's a theory."

Well, I had a theory too.

They were about to have more anguish, more sorrow, than they could handle.

At least my Andrew listened to me when I suggested going to watch the damned creatures first, instead of charging ahead and confronting them.

Men.

"Like a stake out, no?" I asked as we positioned ourselves around the corner from the overly large discount store that had recently opened downtown.

I had no idea why my fellow ghosts were drawn to it, but some were, addicted perhaps to the excitement of shopping, the constant sales and deals the store offered at the start of every hour, like some kind of game show.

The creatures operated a club across the street, private and secure, guarded by muscled thugs in very nice suits. It was on the ground floor of an old office building and had originally been a bar, with custom cocktails and overpriced tidbits. It had never attracted the right clientele and become the hip new joint.

Anyone could have told them the location was all wrong. If they'd opened up a type of dive bar, they'd still be going strong.

Andrew had brought Betsy, his camera, tonight. Her pictures showed the true soul of a place. I know Andrew thought of her as merely some sort of spectralgraph, only showing places where ghosts stayed, but she was much, much more.

Or maybe he did know, as he protected and coddled her as much as he did me.

Fortunately, I was not the jealous type.

I still had to ask, "So what does the other woman see?"

Andrew shook his head but didn't say anything, merely showing me the photos he'd taken.

The office building was all lit up, like St. Michael's on a holy day.

Then he showed me a picture of the street, empty of people, but with weird line, like ropes of Christmas lights, running from the mega store to the clubhouse.

"Their sweet anguish?" Andrew asked, pointing them out.

The next picture showed the store itself, with weird bright portals, lined with strange, spiky energy.

"Wouldn't a hospital be better?" I asked. "Or—where they hold funerals?"

He shrugged. "Maybe there's more constant misery here. Plus, hospitals and funeral parlors have too many counter measures, discouraging ghosts from sticking around. The store, well, it seems to have few defenses."

"Ah, my Andrew. So smart," I told him.

If we'd been alive, I would have kissed him.

As it was, we merely shared a long gaze.

I always wondered at God's plan, to show me such Heaven while in the midst of such Hell.

"There's one," I finally said, breaking the spell between us and looking over his shoulder.

Andrew turned, already snapping away, trusting his Betsy to focus on what was important.

I was right to call them creatures, instead of dignifying them with a name.

Unnatural light spilled from the man, like a wound from Beyond. Lines of sticky magic danced all around him as well, tickling the lines from the store, like an octopus pulling itself along.

Andrew looked disturbed as well. "So we know how they feed," he hazarded.

"Oh yes," I said, nodding. "And I think I know how to poison the well."

IT WAS NOT DIFFICULT TO CONVINCE THE DRIVERS OF THE black cabs that they had a new rival in town.

They had also noticed the decrease in their ledgers.

So I may have stretched the truth a bit—equating the damned creatures need for anguish with the actual ghost "lives" that the cabbies took, so they wouldn't take an accidental one.

The cabbies believed, though.

I may have also promised them more ghosts at their track for their help.

Of course, my Andrew didn't need to know any of that.

He did arrange the meeting though, of Rachel, ourselves, and the creatures, in neutral territory. I'd heard of such places, of course, but I'd never had cause to use one.

I didn't want Andrew to accompany us, but even if I had managed to leave him behind somehow, he still knew the place and time, and would have shown up eventually, angry and vengeful.

While I planned to scare the creatures, I needed to do it a different way.

The location was more perfect than even I could have

planned for: A restaurant that opened its doors after hours for both ghost and men, some kind of gathering place that many used.

Since it was a human-owned restaurant, I assumed the living mostly arranged these meetings as well. Maybe they wanted to talk with us, convince us of something.

We'd never go seek them.

The restaurant was at the corner of a mall out in Woodinville. It was built out from the rest of the buildings, almost on its own peninsula, an octagonal shaped, blandly beige building with floor to ceiling windows on all sides.

As I said, perfection.

I had Manny bring us there.

When Rachel asked about the cab, I passed it off. "A favor repaid from a friend of a friend," I told them.

Manny nodded his turbaned head silently, and I knew if I could see his face, he would have had his own death's head grin.

When we got out, Andrew looked around, quickly accessing the location.

"Long way back to Seattle," he murmured, quietly, so that only I would hear him.

"Manny will wait," I told him dismissively.

"You will tell me later," he whispered as we walked in.

I shrugged, but I knew he was right.

We shared too much for me not to share this secret as well. But later, much, much, later.

The creatures were already there. The staff had put together tables at the center of the restaurant for us.

Directly above, the ceiling sloped higher, and a second set of windows held up a small, octagonal section. There was too much light to see through those windows, but I imagined that some nights it must be lovely with the moonlight slanting through.

Though nothing was being served tonight, the restaurant

still smelled of warm coffee and the fish special they advertised next to the door.

Three of the creatures sat on the far side of the cheap wooden table. They hadn't bothered to take off their black overcoats, that looked like stylized versions of the ones worn in World War II.

They were the palest living things I'd ever seen. Or maybe they, too, prided themselves on idiotic racial purity.

They did stand, though, when they saw that Manny had followed us in.

"What's he doing here?" The short one asked. He had a skull and crossbones tattooed on the back of the hand he pointed with.

Andrew glanced behind him, then turned back to the tables. "He's our ride. Sit down," he growled.

I didn't not let my pride show on my face, but my Andrew's ghostly voice was lovely and chilling.

The three idiots remained standing, though the hand of the one pointing did tremble a little.

Of course, they must have been wearing special earplugs or something, that filtered out most of the ghostly undertones.

"We're not afraid of you," said the middle one quietly, the one looking most unaffected.

Probably the leader.

I came forward quickly and sat down opposite him.

"No, no, of course not. And you should not be. We are no threat. Come." I gestured for the other two to sit.

They came, reluctantly, but they came.

The humans smirked at each other after we'd all sat, leaving them standing, their heads towering above us, like teachers before shrinking school children.

"Please," I said, indicating with my hands that they should sit.

The leader sat first, followed by his two minions.

"You asked for this meeting. Said you might have some news. Something to trade."

"Did you bring it? Yakob Goldman's painting?" I asked him pointedly.

"We disposed of that painting long ago," he said smoothly.

"You did what?" Rachel squeaked. "To whom? When?"

"I can't be bothered with such details," he claimed, dismissing her with a wave of his hand.

Did he lie? It was impossible to know with this one, who lied as easily as breathing.

Luckily, that was how I lied as well, though I no longer needed the breath.

"Are you certain?" I asked. "You may need it."

He shrugged beautifully, such a precise gesture of disregard and insolence.

"You may need to remember," I told him gently. "We are not here merely for us."

Manny stepped forward.

At least the creatures could see enough of the cabbie's mania to be wary.

"What trick is this?" the leader demanded.

I took it as a good sign that he hadn't jumped again to his feet.

"You take from the ghosts. Their anguish and sorrow, yes?" I asked.

The leader grunted, impassive, not agreeing or disagreeing.

"The cabbies take from the ghosts too. Only they give rides in exchange for our terror. You? Are parasites. And feeding from too thin a harvest."

The leader looked puzzled, then shrugged again. "What do you expect us to do about it?"

He was right to be so dismissive. They were protected from my kind: We couldn't even touch them.

I turned to look at Manny.

He nodded.

LEAH CUTTER

Suddenly, the darkness outside the windows was shattered with dozens of headlight, all on bright.

"You can leave," I told the creatures sweetly. "It is not us that you need to fear. But them. They will haunt you on every street. Drive you off every road. Chase you on any bus. You will never be safe until you leave."

Fortunately for me, they were city creatures. They understood what I meant.

Cabs were everywhere. If all the cab drivers suddenly turned against these creatures, there would be nowhere to hide. Every time they left the club or their homes, they'd be hunted.

The leader looked at his two minions, but neither of them seemed to have any answers.

"You may not make it out of Seattle alive, tonight, if you are still carrying Yakob Goldman's painting," I added. "Do you remember the details now?"

The leader regarded me with a calculating eye.

Then Manny stepped forward. "You will remember, and tell my good friend the truth, yes? Or maybe many accidents will happen."

"You bitch," the leader said, finally standing, slamming his hand on the table as he did.

I'd never seen Andrew, or any ghost, move so fast.

He didn't go over or around the table, but *through* it, getting a hair's breath away from the face of the leader. "Watch your language," he warned.

He was threatening enough to give a ghost chills.

I will say this: The creature faced my Andrew without backing down.

"We don't have the painting," he said distinctly, without a tremor in his voice. Then he turned and looked at Rachel. "We never did."

"Then who does?" Rachel asked, standing.

I looked at her, worried. My Andrew could be trusted to

reign himself in, and the leader could probably control his frightened minions.

Rachel, though, was too close to despair to be trusted.

The leader shrugged. "We just used it. We don't actually need *things*," he said disdainfully.

Rachel moaned.

Andrew and I exchanged looks. He was as concerned as I.

I stood and stepped directly in front of Rachel. "No," I told her. "Not here. Not now."

Rachel continued to moan.

Very slight tremors tickled my toes.

"Do not do this," I warned.

I did not know what would happen if she continued. Maybe she would bring the roof down on all of us, or maybe the earth would just shift, and she would shatter all the windows.

I could pay to fix it, of course, but I couldn't pay to fix my reputation in the community, ruining a meeting place like this.

I did the only thing I knew to do—I passed directly *through* Rachel.

Going through a table, or even a car, was disturbing. It felt *wrong* in a way, like deliberately stepping into pond scum when fresh water flowed just a few feet away, or standing on solid earth that turned into cream.

It started Rachel enough to get her to stop.

And it had one other benefit as well: It disturbed whatever tie or spell those creatures had set on her.

Rachel shook herself, as if walking into a warm room after a chilling evening.

The mad whirl of her eyes calmed.

I didn't know how the creatures knew what had happened. Either they'd seen the effect before, or they'd been feeding from her, even here.

"Go," I told them. "Leave. And be prepared to be haunted."

While there were few ghosts I would call selfless, none would let such creatures flourish, now that we knew how to disrupt their spells, take away their prey regardless of their spells.

These creatures were about to be ousted from every city where they had a club, and haunted to death in many.

They deserved nothing better.

It was easy to convince Rachel to step Beyond, now. I was surprised a Portal hadn't sprung up at the restaurant, as soon as her path was clear. Those creatures had taken her away from Heaven.

I hoped endless Hell awaited all of them.

Rachel decided to go to a nearby cemetery to cross over. I didn't go with her. Such a thing is private, no?

It wasn't because I was ashamed of my own Hell, though such things should be private too.

As black as my Andrew's Hell was, belching smoke and fire, mine was white: Empty of trees, sky, people, wine, laughter, or sorrow. It was nothingness I feared, a wasteland without thought, deed, God, or purpose.

I didn't fear my Hell, not really. I knew what waited for me, that I would accept it when my Andrew found his Heaven, as he was sure to.

Though I did sometimes wonder if Hell was actually here. So close to the one I loved, a Heaven in his arms that I would never know.

I thought of these and other fancies only at certain times, like when the dark of the night was overtaken with the dawn and the howling of Hell told me to flee.

Or when I stood in the center of a track, facing down a madman in a cab, letting him take a little piece of me so that others may ride.

ABOUT THE AUTHOR

Leah Cutter writes page-turning fiction in exotic locations, such as a magical New Orleans, the ancient Orient, Hungary, the Oregon coast, rural Kentucky, Seattle, Minneapolis, and many others.

She writes literary, fantasy, mystery, science fiction, and horror fiction. Her short fiction has been published in magazines like *Alfred Hitchcock's Mystery Magazine* and *Talebones*, anthologies like Fiction River, and on the web. Her long fiction has been published both by New York publishers as well as small presses.

Find Leah's books here.

Follow her blog at www.LeahCutter.com.

Reviews

It's true. Reviews help me sell more books. If you've enjoyed this story, please consider leaving a review of it on your favorite site.

Come someplace new...

Are you a traveler? Do you enjoy exploring strange new worlds, new cultures, new people?

Journey into the various lands envisioned by Leah Cutter.

Sign up for my newsletter and I'll start you on your travels with a free copy of my book, *The Island Sampler*.

I will never spam you or use your email for nefarious purposes. You can also unsubscribe at any time.

http://www.LeahCutter.com/newsletter/

ABOUT KNOTTED ROAD PRESS

Knotted Road Press fiction specializes in dynamic writing set in mysterious, exotic locations.

Knotted Road Press non-fiction publishes autobiographies, business books, cookbooks, and how-to books with unique voices.

Knotted Road Press creates DRM-free ebooks as well as high-quality print books for readers around the world.

With authors in a variety of genres including literary, poetry, mystery, fantasy, and science fiction, Knotted Road Press has something for everyone.

Knotted Road Press
www.KnottedRoadPress.com

www.ingramcontent.com/pod-product-compliance
Lightning Source LLC
Chambersburg PA
CBHW070954120726
47910CB00004B/1237